THROUGH THE STORM

Through the Storm

By

PHILIP GIBBS

THE RYERSON PRESS ~ TORONTO

First Canadian Edition

PRINTED AND BOUND IN CANADA
BY THE RYERSON PRESS, TORONTO

THROUGH THE STORM

PART I

FRANCE

I

BEING A NEUTRAL at that time in a World War Edward Hambledon did not feel perturbed for his own personal safety when the Germans reached the Channel ports and had an open road to Paris. As an American, with an American passport, his life and liberty were not endangered.

But things were getting uncomfortable, and for many of his friends and all France terrifying. Terror struck them suddenly. Paris had remained extraordinarily confident and calm even after the enemy had smashed through the French lines opposite Sédan and when their armoured divisions were driving to Boulogne.

"It was worse in 1914," said an elderly man looking after a bookstall on the left bank of the Seine. "Weygand will strike at the psychological moment, as Foch did on the Marne. It is an easier job to cut through that column and join hands with the English. We wait for Weygand, who will strike at the right moment."

"Doubtless that will happen," answered Edward Hambledon of Boston, Massachusetts, who had been two years in Paris as a student of painting and spoke French with an American accent.

In his own mind he was not sure that it would happen. Bill Smart, of the American Embassy, had given him the low-down about the military situation when they had walked through the Tuileries Gardens under a sky full of stars and in the beauty of a perfect night—so beautiful that Hambledon, with an artist's eye, felt its enchantment, with the emerald green grass flooded by moonlight, and the long wings of the Louvre in a black shadow world, and the statues of nymphs gleaming white where they stood. Paris, thought this young American, had never been so wonderfully beautiful as in these days and nights when the fate of France hung in the balance.

Bill Smart had told him that Weygand had gone *gaga* and sat in his headquarters with his head in his hands, incapable of action. The French army was demoralized from top to bottom. There was no decisive command. There was no stopping the massed fury and terror of German tanks and dive bombers. It was beyond human resistance. And the French army and nation, said Bill Smart, had been betrayed for years by corrupt politicians—a stinking and almost incredible corruption—as now they were betrayed by incompetent generals, among whom were Fascist traitors. "France is sunk," said Bill Smart. "Within a week we shall hear the tramp of German boots in Paris. It fills me with horror."

But Paris had remained strangely and heroically calm waiting for Weygand, until, suddenly, terror took hold of everyone. It was as though everyone knew by some mental telepathy that Weygand would not attack, and that defeat was inevitable, and that Paris would soon be in the hands of the enemy.

To Edward Hambledon the first sign of panic came when the concierge and his wife came into his studio on the Boulevard St. Germain at a fantastically early hour in the morning when he was in his dressing-gown before shaving. "M'sieur," said Jean Meunier, the concierge, "excuse us. But we are leaving Paris. It is none too soon."

Edward's hand strayed automaticilly to his cigarette-case on the little table within reach of his pillow and he lit a *petit caporal*. "More bad news?" he asked.

The concierge, a grizzled veteran of the last war—he had fought at Verdun—raised his wrinkled hands with a gesture of despair.

"They will be here in Paris," he said. "Those *sales Boches!* Paris is without defence. *Crê nom de Dieu!*" His body was convulsed by a kind of strangled sob and he turned his head for a moment as though to hide tears.

"It is because of Yvonne that we go," said Madame Meunier. "She is eighteen. We dare not let her stay in Paris until the Germans come. We have to abandon everything. We can take nothing. Perhaps death for all of us would be the best."

Jean Meunier turned to her angrily. "Do not talk such words, Marie. We must think only of Yvonne."

"There is nothing but agony before us," cried Madame Meunier. She clasped her hands together and flinging them with her body against the wall of Edward's studio wept convulsively.

From the kitchen below stairs came a young voice. "*Maman!*"

It was Yvonne, who had often posed for Hambledon in this studio.

He went over to Madame Meunier for whom he had respect and affection, though she had a sharp tongue and had been angry with him many times for rousing her husband in the small hours of the morning when he had come back from late parties. But she had mothered him when he had had the *grippe*, and sewn on his buttons, and swept out his studio, and given him motherly advice about bad women and other perils lying in wait for young men in Paris, and especially, she thought, for young Americans.

He put his arms about her. "Courage!" he said. "Courage, Madame. All is not lost yet, I hope."

"For us it is all lost," she answered more calmly, wiping her eyes with her black apron. She held his hands tight. "For you it does not matter," she said. 'You are an American. The Americans are very lucky. They are far from Hitler and all his devils."

"Where are you going, and how will you go?" asked Hambledon. "I should like to be of help to you."

It was Jean Meunier who answered. "We are taking the train to Tours, if we can fight our way on to it. My wife has a brother there. He will give us house room in his baker's shop."

He turned to his wife and gripped her arm. "It is time we went, Marie. We have only an hour for the train."

Edward felt in his pocket-book and pulled out a wad of notes which he held out to the concierge. "This may help you, old man."

"No, no, m'sieur," said the concierge. But his hands closed round the notes. "A thousand thanks," he said, "and good luck. Now, Marie—"

Madame Meunier clasped Edward's hands in her own.

"Adieu!" she said. "Remember us now and then. We shall think of you often, if we are not killed by the Germans."

She kissed the back of his right hand and then followed her husband out of the room. A few moments later Yvonne came to say good-bye. She had been weeping and her eyes were still wet.

She flung her arms round Edward's neck. "Adieu!" she cried with a sob. "It is terrible, all this."

He felt her young body against his. 'Good luck, my dear," he said. "Keep safe."

She had made love to him now and then and at other times had been very cheeky with him. Once she had told him that he would never be a good painter. He painted atrociously, she said, being an American. No American could be a good artist, because Americans had no souls but only dollars.

Now she wept in his arms and spoke despairingly.

"I shall not be safe. German soldiers will see to that. We shall, of course, all starve to death in any case. It will not be amusing, this life under the Germans."

Hambledon helped this family to get away with their bags and bundles. He drove them to the Gare du Midi, and helped to carry their luggage to the platform. The station was besieged by refugees, all struggling to get away. There was no excitement or outward emotion, but a kind of quiet desperation. Children sat among the baggage, some of them white-faced and frightened, but others unconscious of the terror advancing on Paris and happy with their toys. Their mothers looked haggard and anxious but none wept.

Edward Hambledon watched this scene and the faces of these Parisians. During his two years in Paris he had not limited his experience to the rowdy set of would-be artists and intellectual charlatans and *poseurs* at the Dôme and Rotonde, or to mixed parties of Americans in Montparnasse and Fontainbleau. He had sat at the *zinc*, in cheap little *bistros* round about les Halles getting into friendly conversation with broad-shouldered porters from the markets and young, thin-faced mechanics from garages, and soldiers on leave with their girls.

He had made friends with small shopkeepers from whom he bought his bread and coffee and socks and canvases. He had found them all friendly and intelligent folk, cynical about their politicians—a dirty crowd, they thought, with the exception of Heriot and Blum and a few others. They had been against the war before it came.

"Anything is better than war," said most of them. "France cannot fight another war after all the slaughter and ruin of the last."

When the war came the porters of les Halles took it sullenly.

"England has dragged us in," they said. "It is, of course, the same old war in defence of Capitalism. Our sons will again be the victims of international financiers and of those who play power politics."

During the long period of the "phoney" war as Hambledon's friends called it—for more than half a year there was no serious fighting—some of them had lowered their voices and spoken words which made Edward raise his eyebrows slightly and have an inward doubt about French will-power to defend their liberties.

"We must make an arrangement with those Germans. Cannot we find some way of peace before the slaughter begins?"

Now the slaughter had begun, and French weakness had been revealed, and the Maginot line—which was only half a line—had been turned and ignored by the invading hordes, now pouring in a tide of metal through the French lines, blasting their way on to the heart of France. Paris was being abandoned by its citizens, by all those who could get away somehow and anyhow.

"One can't imagine this ever happening in New York or Boston," thought Edward Hambledon. "We are lucky in our geographical position. Nothing will ever hit us like this."

II

HAVING SAID GOOD-BYE again to the Meunier family, Edward drove back to his studio and found the telephone ringing.

A girl's voice spoke to him when he lifted the receiver. She spoke in French with a perfect accent, though she was Russian. He answered her in French, at which sometimes she had laughed because of his American intonation.

"It's nice to hear your voice again, Olga. You used to ring me up like this before you broke my heart."

He heard her give a faint laugh and a little sigh. "Oh, it has healed again, dear Edouard. There are so many pretty girls who are fond of you."

'I'm not particularly fond of them," answered Edward. "I fell in love with you. Have you forgotten?"

He spoke lightly with a smile in his voice, though she had broken his heart, or he thought she had, when she told him she was going to live with Paul Simon because he played Chopin so exquisitely, and because he needed her more than Edward, being so delicate and sad and tortured.

"I shall always remember our friendship with affection," said the voice on the telephone, that Russian girl's voice which had been sweet music to Edward's ears when he was deeply in love with her.

"It is because of our friendship, dear Edouard, that I want to see you this morning. I want to see you now, in a few minutes. It is because of Paul. I am frightened about him."

"Yes, I suppose he's scared," said Edward Hambledon.

There was another faint sigh on the telephone.

"He remembers that he has a Jewish ancestry. The Germans do not like people with Jewish ancestry even though they have music in their souls. Paul is in great danger. I want to see you about him. I want to ask your help, Edouard. I will be with you in ten minutes if you will wait."

"Certainly I will wait," answered Edward. "But I don't pull any strings, and everybody is rushing away from Paris."

"It is terrible," cried Olga. "I weep for France. Paris is panic-stricken today. I can see fear in the people's eyes. They look like hunted animals, with the hunters very near. . . . In less than ten minutes, Edouard, I will come to you."

In less than ten minutes he heard her tap at his studio.

He saw that she was paler than usual, though her skin had always been rather white, and with her high cheek-bones and her black hair looped over her ears—little shell-like ears which sometimes he had kissed—she looked like one of Leonardo's women.

"It is kind of you to let me come," she said.

"You used to come here many times," he reminded her.

She smiled faintly and looked round his studio with a lingering glance.

"Yes. We had merry times in this room—such gay parties when we all talked such a lot of nonsense. I shall always remember."

"I think of the times when you were here alone with me," said Edward.

She nodded and smiled at him.

"I let you make love to me, Edouard. You were so young and so American. You knew nothing about love. I felt very old because of your young mind and your innocence. I thought it was good for you to love me in a boyish way without any harm in it. Afterwards, you would have a little experience."

"Yes," said Edward with a touch of bitterness, though he laughed. "To you I was just an American schoolboy, very ignorant of life and hardly adolescent. A nice boy to take you out to dinner and drive you to the Bois and send you flowers in the American way."

She looked at him with her dark eyes deeply set under her white forehead.

"Don't think of me unkindly, Edouard. I was very frank with you and very honest. I told you about my lovers—Paul Simon and others. I always laughed when you asked me to marry you. I said I did not snatch babies from their cradles. Do you remember? You cannot accuse me of cheating you. I wanted to be kind to you. I was very glad to let you love me. In any case, all that is in the past, dear Edouard. Let us cherish these memories because they belong to the time of happiness before this war came with all its misery and terror. Are not the Germans advancing on Paris? Shall we not hear the tramp of their boots in a few days, or a few hours?"

She gave a shudder, and looked across the room as though seeing beyond its walls to a horror creeping nearer.

"The Germans in Paris!" she exclaimed in a kind of whisper. "It is unbelievable. Why has it happened like this? Why has France allowed herself to be defeated so soon? Is there not still time to turn the tide?"

"Not a chance," answered Hambledon. "The Germans are too

strong. The French are too weak. Hitler has massed all the metal in the world against them."

Olga turned to Edward and spoke in a quick, urgent way:

"I waste time talking while Paul's life is in danger. There is hardly time to escape. It is why I came here. I want you to find a way of escape for Paul. He is of Jewish parentage. They will put him in a concentration camp where he will die. Or they will shoot him, so that he dies even quicker. It is only you who can help him to escape."

"How?" asked Edward. For just one second he wondered whether it was up to him to help Paul Simon to escape. That thin, delicate, ill-dressed, poverty-stricken fellow had stolen Olga from him. His long, transparent hands had made music which had a magic for her. An American, fresh from Harvard, very young and very callow, had no chance against this consumptive-looking Jew with a lock of black hair over his forehead, and tired eyes. Only for a second this thought came to him. A mean thought.

"Can you get him an American *visa?*" she asked. "If he could get to the United States it would be very wonderful. It would be heaven for him instead of hell. Edouard, because you loved me. . . ."

"What about you?" he asked. "What are you going to do?"

She shrugged her shoulders. "I am a fatalist. I have already been a refugee once. I know the meaning of hunger and lice and a flight from terror. As long as Paul is safe. . . . It may be easier for him to go alone."

"It's not going to be easy," answered Hambledon. "The American Embassy is besieged by would-be emigrants. But I'll do my best for you, Olga; and for Paul Simon, who took you away from me."

"He is very ill," she told him. "He tries to hide his terror. I must go back to him. You will let me know, Edouard?"

He promised to let her know.

Before going she looked round the studio again and her eyes rested on a study he had made of her head.

"It is good, that," she said. "It is alive. It is, perhaps, the best thing you have done."

She did not like many of his other things. Like Yvonne Meunier she thought the American mind was not instinctively in tune with the soul of art. Besides, he was too rich, she thought, to be a good painter. Most of her friends who had talent lived in garrets, ate at cheap restaurants, could hardly afford to buy their canvases and paints, and did not wash very much so that they had the odour of poverty which is the aroma upon which art best thrives. Edward's flow of dollars from a wealthy father in Massachusetts put him in the amateur class, so once she had told him, making him angry.

She turned away from his painting of her head and took his hands and leaned forward and kissed him.

"It is perhaps for the last time," she said. "In any case, it is the last time that I shall come to this room with all its pleasant memories. You will do your best to get Paul away, Edouard, my dear?"

"I will do my best," he answered.

She went away and for a little while he stood quite still thinking about her. He had found her so dainty, and exquisite, and amusing, and wise. She had talked about everything in life with Russian candour, shirking nothing. He had found it exciting and sometimes alarming, this utter frankness of thought and speech. He must have seemed very raw when he first met her in Paris and came to know her. That was in Fontainebleau, where for a time he was a student in the American school of art. Then he had met her in the apartment of Lucile Printemps. Paul Simon had played for them and Edward had seen how spell-bound Olga was by the music. Odd people dropped in to Lucile's apartment—a French novelist, François Denain, who talked bitter stuff about the political corruption of France; a Czech sculptor who looked half-starved and unwashed, but had a touch of genius when he handled his clay; Nancy Stanton, the fashion-writer, who belonged to the rotten set which haunted the Dôme and the Rotonde drinking too many high-balls and throwing overboard all conventions and moralities. Other types dropped in and there had been plenty of talk, most of it in French, and some of it amusing and stimulating to a young man from Massachusetts. He had fallen for the Russian girl, Olga Zhukova.

She had been amused by his boyish love-making, and his shyness, and his free way with dollars. Presently she had let him kiss her. She had reached up to put her fingers through his fair hair. They had walked hand-in-hand through the Bois. Once he had held her in his arms in the shadow of the Louvre under the stars of a Paris night in June.

It was his introduction to love which had ended miserably for him when she went to live with Paul Simon, because, she said, he needed her, being ill and lonely and unhappy. . . . All that was now a memory. The Germans were on their way to Paris. It would soon be the end of Paris and the end of his adventure in that city of enchantment and intellectual liberty.

III

THERE WAS NO DOUBT about the exodus from Paris. Not only was the Gare du Midi besieged by crowds in flight but there was a long tide of cars heading southward from Paris and heavily laden with baggage of all kinds, including perambulators and mattresses and household chattels.

Hambledon crossed this traffic jam in the Rue de Rivoli where it flowed into the Place de la Concorde. A hand came through the window of an old Citroën and a woman's voice spoke to him.

"Aren't you quitting Paris, Edward? I'm just crazy with fear."

It was one of his American friends, Susan Zimmermann, who had been doing fashion drawings for American magazines.

Ernie Zimmermann, her husband, who was news editor of the Paris edition of the *New York Journal*, was driving the Citroën and looked intent on the job while the traffic was held up. Susan was half-buried in baggage, which included a canary in a gold cage which she held on her lap.

She had been one of the hard drinkers at the Dôme where her shrill rasping voice had screamed across the little tables. At the outbreak of war she had stayed on, though most of the American women booked passages home and disappeared from their old haunts. She was one of the few left in a desert of empty chairs outside the Dôme. Now she was making a get-away while there was still time.

Hambledon raised his right hand to her and spoke a few words. "I'll meet you sometime in New York, Susan."

The traffic swirled on past the refuge where he stood with the memory of a frightened woman holding a canary in its cage.

The Government offices on the other side of the Hôtel Crillon were being evacuated. Orderlies were bringing out wooden cases and loading them on to military trucks. French naval officers and officials stood about talking in low tones. A line of cars was waiting to take them away.

"The Government is packing up," thought Edward, glancing at them. "Perhaps that has caused the exodus. The Parisians know that Paris is being abandoned."

A dirty old man, with a long scraggy neck above a ragged shirt without a collar, made a sudden demonstration. He raised a clenched fist and shouted out hoarsely:

"We are betrayed. Cowards and traitors! It is you who have caused our downfall. It is always the same. The soldiers of France are betrayed by their filthy politicians. Now you are in flight to save your skins while the people are abandoned."

A gendarme seized him by the arm and led him away, still shouting.

A woman on the kerbstone turned to Edward and spoke in a low voice.

"It is true, all the same, what he says. We have been betrayed."

Hambledon walked to the American Embassy, with its garden going down to the Champs-Élysées. Round by the main entrance there were groups of Americans and a few French women, married perhaps to Americans, and some Jewish-looking people. Edward shouldered his way through them and went up the steps. The hall porter knew him, and when he asked for Mr. Smart shook his head and laughed.

"I guess you'll have to wait, Mr. Hambledon. Mr. Smart has many friends in Paris and they all want to know the best way back to the United States."

He added a few words in a whisper. "It won't be long before the Germans are here. Terrible news is coming in."

"What's the latest?" asked Hambledon.

The porter shook his head. "A lot of rumours," he answered. "Better ask Mr. Smart. Maybe it will all be in the papers tomorrow."

Edward sat in the ante-chamber to William Ryan Smart's room and smoked seven cigarettes while he waited for others to get in first. He knew some of them slightly. They were some of Smart's fashionable friends—several pretty young women, beautifully dressed in the latest Paris models, with rouged lips and finger-nails, though France was sinking into the abyss and the Germans would soon be in Paris. They, too, smoked cigarettes nervously, and crossed and uncrossed their legs, showing their knees, restlessly. One of them was the American wife of a French politician—something in the French Air Ministry. She was sitting nearest to Edward and spoke to him in a low voice.

"Have you heard the news about Leopold? He has surrendered."

Hambledon was startled.

"Say, is that true?"

"My husband told me," she answered. "It is shameful. And the English are in retreat. They are trying to reach the coast before they are cut off. That, too, is a treachery."

Edward shrugged his shoulders.

"After a Belgian surrender that's all they can do, maybe. Still, it's not amusing, all that."

"The end of France is near," said this lady, glancing both ways to see whether she was overheard. "My husband has a *crise de nerfs*. . . ."

"Trying to get back to the United States?" asked Edward.

She nodded.

"I have had enough of France. I have been behind the scenes of political life. I've seen its corruption, its intrigues, its sinks of iniquity.

When they know the awful truth the French people will cry: 'We have been betrayed.' I could have told them that a long time ago. As the American wife of a French politician I feel unclean. If I can get back to Virginia . . ."

Mr. William Ryan Smart's secretary opened his door and said: "Madame Lajeunesse."

It was this lady who had been sitting next to Edward. She rose, nodded to Edward, and went into the next room. She ignored Edward when she came out, and went away with a worried look and deeper lines about her eyes and mouth.

"Mr. Hambledon," said the secretary presently after the seventh cigarette. Edward Hambledon had an eighth out of Mr. Smart's case.

"I can't say I'm enjoying myself," said that gentleman. "No, sir! It's just hell. All these people think I can work miracles. That's not my line of business. I'm no miracle-maker."

"Has Leopold thrown his hand in?" asked Edward.

Smart nodded. "How did you hear? Not that it matters. The papers will have it tomorrow."

He threw his cigarette into the fireplace and groaned.

"I don't care a damn about these Americans stranded in Paris," he said. "But I agonize over the fate of France. France is my spiritual home. It gives me a shudder down the spine when I think of those grim Germans marching to the Arc de Triomphe."

"Too frightful," answered Edward, who loved Paris no less than William Ryan Smart, and had been closer to its heart among its poor citizens.

He came abruptly to the purpose of his visit.

"You say you can't work miracles. Well, I guess you'll have to work one for me."

"Nothing doing, buddy," said Smart firmly.

"I'm asking you for an American *visa* for Paul Simon," said Hambledon. "He's a Jew and doesn't care for concentration camps."

"Paul Simon? That sick-looking guy who plays Chopin like an angel and has the face of John the Baptist?"

"You've said it."

"Olga Zhukova went to share his squalor, didn't she?"

Edward nodded.

"That's why I'm asking you to put a rubber stamp on his passport. It's for her sake, and it's the least I can do."

William Ryan Smart looked at Edward with a grin.

"Darned generous of you, buddy," he said. "Olga led you up the garden path and then let you down. Everybody knew, of course, and was sorry for a nice fresh American boy, as innocent as a spring chicken."

Edward looked annoyed and answered curtly:

"Oh, to hell with everybody. Olga and I remain good friends. Anything you can do about it?"

Smart thought within himself.

"I'll have a word with the Ambassador. He's sympathetic towards Jews."

"Thanks a lot," said Edward.

"Better give me the address of Paul Simon's bug-infested garret," said Smart. "Of course, I can't make any promise."

He held out his left hand, nearest to the heart, in the French style, and Edward gripped it for a moment. William Ryan Smart was a good friend and a regular fellow.

"That's fine," said Hambledon, leaving the room of a hard-pressed young man who yet had time to think of the tragedy of France and bled at the heart for Paris.

IV

EDWARD HAMBLEDON HAD dinner next night in the Père Jean up the rue Montmarte. It was an old haunt of his to which he had gone before the war as an escape from the crowd in Montparnasse, which sickened him now and then because of its noise and insincerity.

Here in the Père Jean he had made friends with the *patron* and his wife, and with their son Bertrand, now in the Army, and with Suzanne, the little waitress, and with Pierre the *garcon* who had married her just before the war when he was called up and put into the Maginot Line as a gunner in one of its steel turrets. Edward had played cards with the *patron* and his wife when most of the customers had gone, and had taught them Gin Rummy and other American card games, letting them win now and then. And in this cheap eating-place with its sanded floor and little tables with cloths of blue and white check he had made friends with the habitués who fed here most evenings.

At the outbreak of war some of them had been called up for military service, like the waiter Pierre. There was a young mechanic from a neighbouring garage with whom Edward had talked politics and from whom he had learned the psychology—rather violent—of the extreme left. He turned up now and again in uniform, being the driver of a General's car at Army headquarters.

Then there was a Russian taxi-driver who had escaped from the Reds with the remnants of Wrangel's army in the Crimea. Like all Russians he liked to talk, and go on talking, and crossed swords good-humouredly on political issues with the garage hand. Now and again he brought in a pretty Russian girl who worked as a sempstress with a dress-making staff of a Grand Duchess in the Place Vendôme. This taxi-driver had dropped his Russian name and called himself Gaston. "My Russian life," he said, "is now nothing but a dream. I am a Parisian. I belong to Paris. I am Gaston Leblanc."

When Hambledon stepped into this place that evening the little restaurant was deserted, except for two of the habitués. One was a little old man who said he was an Englishman and had the English name of Robinson, though he spoke the *argot* of Paris and had lived there all his working life as a newspaper man. He had been on many Paris editions of English and American papers, being sacked from most of them because of an incurable passion for absinthe. From time to time he disappeared, and it was generally understood that he lay in some miserable garret with his absinthe fiend.

Madame Marchand, the wife of the *patron*, passed this off in a delicate way. "M'sieur Robinson has been taken ill again. We shall not see him for a week or two perhaps."

When he reappeared he resumed his normal habits of life, among which was his evening meal at the Père Jean, followed by an unending game of Patience, always at the same table, while he smoked innumerable *Petits Bleus*. He was there that night, playing with his well-thumbed packs of cards, as though nothing threatened Paris or his own way of life.

The other man dining that night at the Père Jean was Louis Duval, who had been a garage hand and now drove a General on the headquarters staff.

As Edward stopped at his table for a moment he raised his head which was low over a bowl of soup and said, "Still here, young fellow?"

His tunic was undone at the neck and there was the white dust of country roads on his bronzed face.

"How goes it, old man?" asked Hambledon.

Louis Duval shrugged his shoulders and laughed without mirth.

"How goes it? It goes fast in the wrong direction. The French army cannot hold a line anywhere. The troops are demoralized for lack of orders, and perhaps for other reasons, such as meeting the fugitives on the roads, and among them their own women and little ones. My General is dining with his mistress tonight. At G.H.Q. the Generals and staff officers have lost touch with the armies. Nothing works. Not even the telephones. They sit stupefied, those Generals and staff officers. But my own General who, of course, should be shot with all the others, dines tonight with his mistress in Paris. She is, very likely, a German spy."

He bent his head again over his bowl of soup.

The elderly Englishman looked up from his cards and nodded to Edward, putting a new cigarette into his holder with a trembling hand due to absinthe.

"Delighted to see you tonight, Hambledon," he said in French. "We are somewhat low in spirit. Being old and sinful I have no fear for my own life. It is always better to be dead. But I grieve for the fate of Paris, my second and kindest mother."

He uttered a frightful oath against Hitler, and then returned to his game of cards, which he dealt out in five rows.

Edward went to the counter, behind which sat Madame Marchand—a plump little woman of middle age with well-combed hair looped over her ears.

"Any news of Bertrand?" asked Edward, holding one of her hands for a moment.

She put her other hand on Edward's and clasped it tight. He could feel a tremor pass through her and there was agony in her eyes. She had worked only for young Bertrand to give him a good education, to set him on a good career, which was to have been the law.

"No word comes," she answered. "It is six weeks since we had his last postcard written from the Maginot Line."

The *patron*, her man, looked up from an evening paper and thrust his leaden-rimmed glasses to the top of his forehead.

"It is probable that Bertrand is alive and unhurt," he said. "The Germans have not attacked the Maginot Line, which, as Bertrand has told us, so often, is impregnable."

Duval, with the dust of country roads on his tanned skin, spoke from his table.

"The Maginot Line is now a farce! The Germans ignore it and attack where it does not exist. It is only half a line. The French people have been deluded about it by their Generals and their politicians and by the daily lies in a paid Press. The Maginot Line is an illusion behind which we felt secure, when there was no security, because of corruption everywhere and unreadiness for war. Daladier was reluctant to declare war but he yielded to the English Chamberlain. It was, of course, the suicide of France."

Marchand, the *patron*, spoke with sarcasm. "You say these things now, Duval. I remember that once you said other things. You were a follower of Leon Blum and his forty hours' week—forty hours when Germany was working day and night to forge the weapons which have now blasted us."

Duval answered sullenly:

"Leon Blum was our only honest man. He may have made a few mistakes. . . ."

Madame Marchand gave an impatient cry.

"Can you still talk politics when we wait for the Germans to enter Paris—when my only son may be dead with so many others—and when Suzanne here is weeping her heart out because her man has been killed in action?"

"That is true," said Marchand. "This is no time for argument."

"Is it true about Pierre?" asked Edward, still standing at the counter.

Madame Marchand nodded.

"One of his friends passed through Paris yesterday in a hospital train. He sent word to Suzanne in a scribbled note by one of the porters who used to come here with Gaston. Pierre was killed at his side."

"I am sorry," said Edward Hambledon, in a low voice.

At that moment Suzanne came into the room from the kitchen, where she had been fetching a dish of tripe for Duval. Her face was very white and blotched by much weeping.

"I am sorry, Suzanne," said Edward.

She pushed the tripe in front of Duval and for a moment her eyes, which once had been so merry, looked like those of a stricken animal. A sob shook her body, but she answered bravely:

"He died for France at a time when most French soldiers are running away."

Duval stared at her sombrely.

"It is all they can do," he said harshly. "They receive no orders. Their battalion officers hear nothing from the high command. No reinforcements arrive. Isolated units fight until they are over-run by German tanks, who drive deep into the heart of France while those poor devils up there do not know where the front is, or what positions they have to defend. All they can do is to fall back. It is not running away. It is falling back to positions already far behind the German advance with its tanks and flame-throwers and dive-bombers. Against all that we are powerless. All the same, I am sorry about Pierre. He and I were good comrades."

Suzanne answered him coldly.

"In a little while we shall all be dead. It makes no difference. This life is unendurable."

"It will be unendurable under the Germans," said Madame Marchand. "But I must stay in Paris until we hear from Bertrand."

Suzanne gave a shrill mirthless laugh.

"In a little while there will be German soldiers seated at these tables. They will ask me to bring them beer. They will make love to me, and then I will throw the beer in their faces and then they will kill me. That is quite an amusing thought!"

Mr. Robinson looked up from his cards and spoke quietly.

"You are too much in terror of the Germans. They are poor dumb beasts, really. Many of them will be well-behaved in Paris. The officers will be correct and try to be civilized. Some of them, no doubt, will have good manners. I have been to Germany now and then."

"Hush!" said Madame Marchand, suddenly. "I hear heavy footsteps."

The *patron* looked up from his paper and listened. Suzanne stopped with a greasy plate in her hand. Duval looked up from his tripe. Old Robinson held a card poised in his trembling hand.

Some time ago the sound of footsteps coming down the rue Montmartre would not have been alarming. There would have been many feet passing ceaselessly, as midinettes, soldiers, workmen, sempstresses, and the frequenters of cabarets and the night life of Paris passed on their way. But tonight there was a sinister silence in this quarter, as in other parts of Paris. The streets were empty.

The footsteps passed the Père Jean.

"*Agents de police*," said Duval.

"It is too soon yet for the others," said the old Englishman, Mr. Robinson. "We are all rather nervous."

The door of the restaurant opened presently as other steps approached and then stopped. Gaston, who once had a Russian name, came in with his pretty girl who helped to make frocks all day in the Place Vendôme.

He nodded to the *patron* and his wife, hung his peaked cap on a peg, and drew out a chair from one of the small tables.

"It is still necessary to eat," he said. "The human animal is like that."

The Russian girl, whom he called Lydia, glanced at herself in one of the mirrors, took off a little hat, and smoothed down her hair. She had sharp cheek-bones and a low broad forehead and heavily rouged lips which accentuated the whiteness of her skin.

"Perhaps it is the last time we shall eat here," she said. "In any case, there may be nothing to eat. The Germans have big appetites. They will take everything."

When Suzanne came up with the bill of fare the Russian girl spoke to her in a whisper.

"It is terrible about Pierre. Gaston has told me. I weep for you."

She took hold of the girl's left hand and raised it to her lips. Suzanne's face became red for a moment and then very white.

"It is, no doubt, kind of you," she said in a sullen voice, "but it won't bring back my man. He is dead. . . . He is lucky. I have an idea that it is best to be dead."

Lydia shook her head and made a little grimace.

"I am fond of life. With all its cruelties life is still precious."

"Tripe or Vienna steak, *mademoiselle?*" asked Suzanne. Lydia chose Vienna steak. Gaston preferred tripe.

"I will have a Dubonnet before eating," he said. He looked over at Edward, who had taken his place at his usual table.

"You stay in Paris?" he asked. "Most of your countrymen have left; and yet, as neutrals, they will not be touched."

"I shan't go yet," answered Edward. "I want to see what is going to happen."

Gaston's lips twisted with a smile, but he answered dryly. "It will not be amusing. Once, when I was a Russian . . ."

"Do not get back to that old dream, Gaston," said Lydia, impatiently.

There was silence in the Père Jean. A few other people came in. One of them was a Chinese student who nodded and smiled to the company as though everything was merry and bright, though his words in queer French were not funny.

"I am very sorry. My heart drips blood. I have a love for Paris."

He gave a shrill little laugh and took a chair at Edward's table. "You permit?" he asked.

A slim, dark-eyed young woman slipped in and sat down alone. She was a dancer at the *Folies Bergères*.

Not long afterwards two other customers arrived. They were Paul Simon and Olga.

It was Olga who saw Edward first. Her eyes roved round the little restaurant until she saw him and raised her gloved hand. She came up to his table and spoke in a low voice.

"I hoped to find you here. Have you good news for Paul?"

"Not yet," said Edward; "But Bill Smart is going to have a word with the Ambassador. He will let me know."

"A thousand thanks to you, Edouard."

"I am grateful," he said. "Olga has told me about your kindness. I live in a nightmare. I am a slave of fear. It is because of my Jewish blood and racial memories of pogroms and massacres. When they come they will find out that I have Jewish ancestry. They will have no mercy. But I am ashamed of being so much afraid."

Edward released his thin, white, long-fingered hand and saw the fear in Paul Simon's eyes.

"Poor devil!" he thought. "He looks like a hunted animal."

"Shall we eat with you, Edouard?" asked Olga.

"Why not?" answered Edward. He glanced at the little Chinese, who sprang up and smiled.

"I go to another table. As Confucius said, 'The stranger must not linger at the hearthside of friends.' "

"It is good of you," said Olga in her charming way.

Paul Simon gave a deep quivering sigh and spoke in a tragic voice.

"Paris is a ghost city tonight. It is a desert. It seems to be waiting for its supreme moment of tragedy."

"I am afraid that is going to happen," said Edward. "Unless a miracle prevents it."

His eyes rested on the face of this man who had cut him out with Olga. It was a striking face, very thin and fine, with a light brown beard and moustache and pale blue eyes, infinitely sad. He had seen the agony of the Jews in Germany and had fled to escape it. Perhaps this racial persecution was always in his subconsciousness; but poverty and ill-health and the torment of genius, hard to get recognized, formed some part of his melancholy. William Ryan Smart had said that he had the face of John the Baptist, but there was not enough fire in him for that.

"I wonder what Olga found in him beyond the need for pity," thought Edward, and glancing towards her he saw that she had noticed his scrutiny of Simon. She coloured up slightly and smiled faintly. She had, of course, worshipped his gift for music.

"Life," she said, "is inexplicable."

Perhaps that was in answer to his unspoken thought.

There were spells of silence in the Père Jean until an argument broke out between Duval—who had driven a General's car—and Gaston the taxi-driver.

"It is you people with foolish ideas about Communism who have brought about the ruin of France," said Gaston. "You wanted higher wages for less work, and thought the State should provide a comfortable life for all. Meanwhile, Germany was arming and Hitler prepared for the domination of Europe, and after that new worlds to conquer."

Duval uttered an oath and laughed harshly.

"You are a white Russian, Gaston, disguised as a French taxi-driver. You have the mentality of your disgusting Grand Dukes and your parasitical aristocrats. Shall I tell you what is going to happen later on? It is because I am a Communist that I know."

"Tell me," said Gaston carelessly. "It is, of course, some fairy-tale. The Left in France has always believed in the fairy-tale of Russian Communism, as though it were a beautiful democracy inspired by the spirit of liberty and human benevolence."

"I will tell you," said Duval. "The Russians and not the Germans will win this war. In the end, after her first victories, Germany will be rolled back by Stalin's Red Armies. France will join hands with her Russian comrades. The workers of Europe will join together to form a United States of free Soviet Republics."

Gaston shrugged his shoulders and answered contemptuously:

"Another fairy-tale! A bad dream!"

Lydia put her hand on his arm as though to check his angry speech.

"I have an idea that Duval may be right," she said. "I hear strange things from Moscow. An American journalist I know who has just come back. . . ."

Gaston looked at her as though she were a child talking nonsense.

"These American journalists spend three days in Paris and then write a book about France," he said. "Is that not so?"

He looked over at the young American but Hambledon did not answer. At that moment the walls of the Père Jean shook, and the floor-boards trembled, and a blast of air seemed to be forcing its way against the windows. There was a heavy reverberating noise like the sound of gunfire, and other explosions followed by crashes of masonry.

"They are coming! They are here!" cried Madame Marchand. She put her hands to her ears and shut her eyes.

There was another violent explosion. Suzanne dropped a pile of plates.

"No, no!" shouted Duval. "It is an air raid. They are bombing the outskirts of Paris."

Mr. Robinson's cards were blown off the table.

Paul Simon had stood up at the first sound of explosion. His face was dead white, and his long thin hands trembled as he touched the table with his finger-tips. "Is this death?" he asked quietly.

"Not yet, I guess," said Edward reassuringly. "They're some way off, I should say."

Olga rose and put her arm round Paul Simon.

"Courage, my dear," she said in a low voice. "Let us not be afraid of death."

Seven bombs fell. The Père Jean shook seven times, as though a giant fist were hammering at its walls.

Overhead there was the drone of planes. Paul Simon took a dirty handkerchief from his pocket and wiped his forehead on which there was a cold sweat.

"You give me courage," he said. "I owe everything to you, Olga—everything in life. I want to tell you that once again."

"I like you to tell me," said Olga. "You have told me a thousand times." She listened intently and then spoke again. "It's quiet now. Let us go home. I will put you to bed."

"No, no!" said Simon. "I am all right. It is only my nerves. They are a little frayed perhaps."

Suzanne stood in the middle of the floor where she had dropped a pile of plates. Suddenly she cried out angrily.

"It is senseless, all this! This war is abominable! Why do we not stop all wars? Why should all our men be slaughtered? Is it not time that men and women in all countries should say, 'We will not make war on each other? We do not want to kill each other. We will not fight in any kind of war?' Have we not enough intelligence for that?"

Nobody answered this outburst for a moment or two. It was Duval in his uniform who answered her.

"One day we shall have that intelligence. That is, when all the workers of the world unite in comradeship."

Suzanne began to sob and, without stooping to pick up the broken plates, went quickly into the kitchen.

"Poor child!" said Olga.

"There is truth in what she said," remarked Gaston. "Why does not mankind use its intelligence to prevent these wars?"

Mr. Robinson answered him, after picking up his cards which had been flung to the floor. "They have no intelligence, my friend. Surely you do not believe in human intelligence?"

The young woman who danced at the *Folies Bergères* spoke for the first time.

"Humanity is disgusting. Man is a filthy animal."

The Chinese student giggled and spoke across the room.

"It has been said by Confucius that man is partly animal and partly spirit. There is no barrier to his spiritual progress if he treads his animal nature beneath his heels."

He laughed happily at this piece of wisdom and then gave a long-drawn sigh.

"It is very silent outside," said the *patron*. "In the rue Montmartre it's as quiet as death."

"It's the death of Paris," said his wife.

Gaston rose to go with the Russian girl. He shook hands with the *patron* and his wife and then with Edward and Duval.

"I am taking Lydia to the south," he said. "It is our last night in Paris for some time. But one day we shall come back. Paris will not die."

"I go too," said Duval. "My General has ordered me for eleven o'clock. He will have had four hours with his pretty slut. I expect I shall be driving him to Bordeaux. The French army is abandoned. The Generals are in flight. Who will pay for this treason?"

V

A LITTLE LATER Olga rose to go back with Paul Simon. "I will walk with you," said Edward Hambledon. They walked into the deserted streets of Paris. Here and there stood *agents de police*. In the dimness of the blackout a few people passed like ghosts. Now and again a car heavily-laden flashed by. Under an archway a soldier embraced a girl, love being stronger than despair. Abandoned cats prowled miserably among the debris of packing-cases in the courtyards.

"Once I have seen Paris gay," said Olga. "Tonight it is a tomb."

As they walked across the Tuileries Gardens to the left bank of the Seine she put her hand on Edward's arm.

"Do you mind?" she asked.

"I like it," he told her. "It reminds me of happier days."

Paul Simon walked ahead of them with nervous steps. He had taken off his hat to feel the cool air on his forehead. Suddenly he stopped and turned round to face them and spoke to Edward.

"Olga tells me that you are being kind and helpful," he said. "It is generous of you, my friend."

"That's quite all right," answered Edward.

"I thank you a thousand times," said Simon. "But I wish to tell you something."

Olga questioned him curiously.

"What is it, Paul? What do you wish to tell Edouard?"

"It is this," said Paul Simon. "I will not leave France without you, Olga. I am not very brave, that is true, but I am not without a sense of honour. If our American friend here can obtain *visas* for you as well as for me that will be excellent. But I will not leave you here alone. That would be infamous after all your care of me. I would rather die in a concentration camp."

Olga gave a little cry.

"I will not let you die in a concentration camp. You must go without me, Paul. We are not married. I cannot come as your wife. The Americans are severe about such things. I have been told that many times. Is it not true, Edouard?"

Edward nodded.

"It is one of our hypocrisies. We are not as virtuous as all that, but make a fetish of the marriage laws even if they are made in Hollywood."

"Is it not possible to get a *visa* for Olga?" asked Paul Simon. "Separately, I mean. We will marry when we get to the United States."

"There are so many would-be refugees," answered Edward. "And time is running short, I'm afraid."

Olga spoke to Paul Simon emotionally.

"Paul, my dear, you must go without me. You will play Chopin in New York and Chicago and I shall be happy knowing you are safe. In any case, I must stay in France. My mother and father are living near Nice. I will join them. I cannot desert them. It was they who carried me away from Russia in the time of Revolution."

"I will not go without you," said Paul Simon, stubbornly.

Olga gave a little cry again.

"Oh, Paul, my dear, do not be obstinate. Have I not given you my love? Do you not owe me something?"

"I owe you everything," answered Simon. "You have sacrificed yourself for me. Now you wish to sacrifice yourself again. In any case, how can I do without you? In America I shall be a lost soul without you."

Olga pleaded with him as though he were a spoilt child.

"Try to be a little reasonable. Is it quite impossible for you to be a little reasonable, Paul? Do you not understand that if you stay in France you will die in a concentration camp? Will that make me happy, do you think? Shall I get any comfort because you stay?"

Paul Simon was silent. Edward watched him as he stood there in the Tuileries Gardens clenching an old felt hat so that the moonlight, very bright and glamorous, revealed his thin delicate face and touched his hair and pointed beard.

"It is not certain that I shall get the *visa*," he said presently. "Everything is uncertain."

Two people passed them—a young man and woman of the working classes. They spoke in low tones, but their words were audible.

"When the Germans come I shall go into hiding," said the man.

"You are mad," said the woman's voice. "You cannot hide for years."

She began to sob quietly and the man put his arm about her as they passed.

"It is the devil who has caught us all," he said.

Edward walked with Olga and Paul to the entrance of the little courtyard on the Ile de France not far from Notre-Dame, where Paul had a room.

"Come in for a little while," said Olga.

"No," said Edward. "I must get back. We may hear something tomorrow."

Paul Simon gripped his hand.

"I am not ungrateful," he said. "You are very kind to a poor dog of a Jew."

"*Au revoir*, *cher Edouard*," said Olga.

When he took her hand she lifted up her face to this tall American, and then put her arm round his neck and laid her cheek against his for a moment. Her cheek was wet and her tears were on his lips when he kissed her.

VI

CHAS HUNT, who represented an American journal in Paris, thrust his head out of a taxi-cab in the Boulevard St. Michel and hailed Edward Hambledon, who was reading the headlines of the *Petit Parisien*.

Surrender of the Belgians. British Retreat to Dunkirk.

"Hullo, Edward!"

"Good morning," answered Edward, curtly. He had heard that grim news before. Now it was officially confirmed.

The taxi-cab slowed down at the kerbstone and Chas Hunt spoke again with a kind of urgency.

"Say, Edward, I've hired this Jehu to push out from Paris and get as near as he dare to the Front. Care to take a chance and come along? We may see something of the real thing—anyhow, the back-wash of it."

"Why don't you drive your own car?" asked Edward, giving himself time to think out this offer.

Chas Hunt laughed without amusement.

"Somebody pinched it yesterday. Probably it's being driven to Nice or Bordeaux by some hound of hell."

"I'll come with you," said Edward.

"Fine!" exclaimed Chas Hunt, a hard-boiled newspaper man, once of Kansas City, tall, lean-jawed, and steely-eyed. "I like a guy of quick decision. Come inside this bone-rattling box of tricks."

He called to the taxi-driver:

"*En avant!*"

The driver was a middle-aged man with a grey moustache and a three-days' growth of stubble on his chin. He looked haggard and nervous.

"*Messieurs*," he said, turning in his seat, "I do not guarantee anything. If you wish to risk your lives that is no concern of mine, you understand?"

"Perfectly, old man," answered Chas Hunt. "But we do not wish to get killed or taken prisoner. That also is understood."

He spoke French like Edward, fluently, but with an American intonation not to be disguised.

"For myself it does not matter," said the driver. He didn't give a curse about death, he said. He explained that he had a daughter with a new-born babe in Dieppe. He might find her on the road with other refugees if he pushed up that way. That is why he had consented to go.

"Well, now that we thoroughly understand each other, shall we make a start?" asked Chas Hunt impatiently.

They drove through the outer suburbs, which became miserable and squalid, with rows of dilapidated houses and small shops and rubbish heaps. Few people were about and those looked gloomy and frightened.

Presently the taxi left Paris behind, taking the road from Evreus to Pontoise. It passed through a pleasant countryside with meadows bordered by willow trees and ditches tangled with wild flowers. Here and there were glimpses of small châteaux with mansard roofs half-hidden beyond avenues of tall trees. They passed through villages silent and deserted as though the inhabitants had all fled.

Edward stared out of the cab at the passing scene, very lovely in the fresh foliage of Spring. French poets of the sixteenth century had put these wild flowers in their sonnets. They had made love to the ladies of France in parklands like these. Edward knew this part of the road getting near to Pontoise. He had driven Olga out here one afternoon and she had made a daisy chain and crowned him as he lay at her feet in a quiet meadow.

The driver of this Paris taxi seemed to be moved by this pastoral beauty. He turned in his seat and spoke to Edward over his shoulder.

"The beauty of France!" he exclaimed in a tragic voice. "It is horrible, *M'sieur*, that the Germans will soon be all over this countryside."

"I agree," said Edward with sympathy.

Chas Hunt was not observing the loveliness of Nature. He had some other thought in his mind, to which presently he gave expression.

"Where is the French army? Where, in God's name, are the troops and guns who ought to be here defending Paris? This is the straight road to Paris and there are no defences, that I can see."

"Paris will not be defended," said the taxi-driver. "We have already lost the war. There is no hope for us."

Chas Hunt turned to Edward with a kind of stupefaction in his eyes and spoke in English.

"They've just packed up. God knows what has happened to them. It's a moral *débâcle*."

"They've been betrayed by their leaders," answered Edward. "I guess when that happens the rank and file lose heart."

Farther along the road the two friends saw a group of about fifteen soldiers. They were sitting on a bank above the road in a listless, hang-dog way. A young lieutenant was standing up, and stared at the taxi as it approached.

"I'm going to speak to those guys," said Chas Hunt. He told the taxi-driver to stop and got out. Edward followed him and saw him touch his felt hat to the young lieutenant, who raised his hand to his steel helmet.

"What is the situation?" asked Chas Hunt in his fluent French with a strong American accent.

The young lieutenant, who was a good-looking man, though unshaven for several days, shrugged his shoulders slightly as he answered.

"There is no situation. It is chaos. The English are fighting in Dieppe to cover the retreat of their army to Dunkirk."

"Where is the French army?" asked Hunt.

The lieutenant looked at him sombrely.

"They, too, are cut off in the north."

"But here?" asked Hunt. "Why is Paris left undefended? Why are there no troops or guns across this road?"

"I have not the honour of being in the headquarters of General Weygand," answered the young officer coldly.

"It is incredible!" exclaimed Hunt.

The lieutenant spoke suddenly with extreme bitterness and passion.

"Certainly it is incredible! Those who were killed at Verdun and in other fields of France must turn in their graves when they think of all that sacrifice, the sacrifice of two million comrades, wasted by what now happens. We allowed the Germans to get strong again. Our politicians sank into corruption. Like pigs they wallowed in their filth. They did not provide the weapons. Some of our Generals were politicians also, and many of our men are Communists. They have not the will to fight. Those who have the will to fight do not get any orders. I have been left for two days without an order, and stay here with an anti-aircraft gun, not knowing what to do or where to go."

"*Mon lieutenant*," said one of the men, standing up from his seat on the bank. "I can tell you what to do and where to go. These gentlemen have a taxi-cab. They will take us back to Paris. We can sit on each others' laps and even on the roof. I have a woman in Paris. I wish to see her again."

"Shut your beak," said the French lieutenant sternly.

Another man rose from the bank.

"I am a married man," he said. "I do not wish to be taken prisoner when those swine spill all over the countryside. We are abandoned. It is useless to stay here. I agree with Jean Bernard that Paris is better than this green grass. From Paris one may get a train somewhere."

"Shut your beaks," said the young lieutenant. "You have my orders to stay."

Another man rose and spat in the grass before speaking.

"You are a child, *mon lieutenant*," he said harshly. "We older men have more sense in our heads. We also have wives and children. We no longer obey your orders, *mon lieutenant*. We do not care a curse for them."

"If you go I will have you shot as a deserter," said the young lieutenant.

The man, who was a bull-necked, broad-shouldered fellow, laughed gruffly.

"All that is over," he said. "The French armies do not exist. The German tanks have driven deep and there are no lines. It is not desertion to escape being captured. It is common sense."

"It is the best idea," said one of the others. They rose and talked among themselves.

The young lieutenant turned his back on the men and spoke to the two Americans.

"Where are you gentlemen going? They are bombing the villages beyond Pontoise, and the roads are choked with refugees."

As he spoke there was the noise of heavy explosions, perhaps three kilometres away.

"I should like to get a bit farther on," said Chas Hunt. "As a newspaper man . . ."

The taxi-driver spoke to the young officer.

"*M'sieur*, you say there are refugees on the roads. It is possible that my daughter is among them. She had a little flower-shop in Dieppe."

"My poor fellow!" said the young lieutenant, "it is like looking for a needle in a bundle of hay. There are swarms of refugees on the roads. A long column passed yesterday, ten kilometres long. Another has already passed this morning, taking the road southwards. It is a distressing sight, all those women and children and the old people."

A sudden mist of tears came into the eyes of the taxi-driver and he smudged them away with the back of his hand.

"Would that I had been killed at Verdun," he said in a broken voice. "They were lucky who were killed in the last war!"

"Would you care to come with us, *mon lieutenant?*" asked Chas Hunt. "We could give you a lift back even as far as Paris."

The young officer looked at him uncertainly and then glanced at his men, who were talking together in low voices.

"I shall be glad to come with you a little way," he said. "Perhaps as far as Pontoise. As a matter of fact, I belong to this region. My family has a little château fifteen kilometres farther back towards Paris, away from the main road. I am anxious about them, you understand. They may have gone, of course. The last time I saw my father he talked of sending them to our farmhouse near Tours, though he had decided to stay and wait events."

He introduced himself as Armand de Rollencourt.

He spoke a few words to one of his men and then came back to the taxi.

"Step in, lieutenant," said Chas Hunt.

VII

It was some miles beyond Pontoise when they met another tide of refugees and had to pull on to the grass by the side of the road. It was a long tide of farmcarts with slow-moving horses and covered wagons and tradesmen's carts, and rusty bicycles ridden by young boys, and a long trail of village folk on foot. They were of all ages. Very old women were perched among their chattels and mattresses piled high on the farmcarts. They wore their Sunday black and little black bonnets, and their old wrinkled faces—the grandmothers of France—were whitened by the dust of the road. Young women of sturdy peasant stock trudged along, carrying their babies, with older children holding their hands or skirts. Old men, who had ploughed the fields of France, walked with heavy feet. Some of them had bundles on their shoulders. Others were trundling wheelbarrows heaped up with baggage and oddly-shaped bundles. Some of them walked hand-in-hand with small children. They were all dusty, hot and footsore, and sweat trickled down their faces, and the white dust of the roads made their eyes look darker. They had tragic eyes filled with anguish because of the flight from their homes and their belongings with the enemy on their heels.

"This is the saddest side of war," said Armand de Rollencourt. "These poor people! They are like frightened sheep with the wolves behind them."

The taxi-driver stood on the edge of the road staring at these people hungrily. He was searching for his daughter among them. Several times he went over to speak to them and Edward heard his words.

"I am looking for my daughter, Odette. You know her, perhaps? Madame André. She has a little flower-shop in Dieppe."

No one had seen her.

The long column, stretching back for several kilometres, came to a halt. Some of the farm-horses were overtired and could plod on no farther without a rest. Some of the refugees left the road and lay down upon the grass at its side—long grass tangled with wild flowers. Some of them fell asleep instantly, having walked for several days and nights without rest. Babies were squealing. Young mothers sitting on the grass held them to their breasts and fed them. Young girls, more smartly dressed than the peasant women, combed their hair in the sun and used their handkerchiefs to wipe the dust off their faces.

Armand de Rollencourt gave a cry of astonishment and spoke to one of these girls.

"Madeleine! Good God! Why are you here? It is terrible to see you here like this."

She had been sitting down on the grass but sprang up at the sound of his voice and the sight of him.

"Oh, Armand! Certainly it is terrible. I was staying with Aunt Claire in Dieppe. We did not think the Germans would come so quickly. There was an English officer who was billeted with my aunt. He said the enemy would never get to the coast. My aunt refused to come. She has now been taught by the Germans."

It was ten minutes later when the taxi-driver suddenly made a rush across the road. He gave a loud cry.

"Odette! My poor daughter! My beautiful Odette!"

By some miracle he had found his daughter in this crowd—a slim girl with neatly braided hair and a little white collar round the neck of her black frock. She carried a new-born babe in her arms. At the sight of her father she ran a little way and then clung to him.

Edward Hambledon spoke in a low voice to Chas Hunt.

"I'm darned sorry for all these people."

"It makes me want to burst into tears," answered Hunt. "I'm a hard-boiled newspaper man, but I still have bowels of compassion."

He did not burst into tears. He stared up at the sky, cloudlessly blue, and was interested, intensely interested, in a black speck coming nearer. In another second or two it looked like a black hawk in the blue dome.

"I don't like the look of that," said Hunt. "It's an enemy plane."

The head of the column had begun to get on the move again. Old cart-horses strained in their shafts and plodded on with their heavy loads. Some of the boys had mounted their bicycles. Old men stooped to their wheelbarrows.

The distant hum in the sky, like a homing bee, became a louder drone. Some of those who had been lying on the grass sprang to their feet and looked upwards. Everybody was staring at that black hawk. An old man, with a thin bare neck showing his Adam's apple, raised a clenched fist at it and shouted a French oath.

Suddenly the black hawk flew low. There was the roar of its engines and a rush of wind over the heads of the crowd. Many flung themselves down on the road and grass. Distinct from the roar of the low-flying plane there was another sound, like nails being hammered into a coffin by some demon carpenter. It was the rat-tat-tat of a machine-gun.

Chas Hunt had flung himself on to the grass with the others, but Hambledon stood still. For some reason, inexplicable to himself, he was unable to move and seemed to have been turned to stone. His soul had been turned to stone, it seemed. He saw a woman fall dead, face forwards, with her arms outspread. He saw a boy on a bicycle lurch sideways and then fall with his face in the white dust, and scarlet blood coming from a hole in his head making a pool in the road. He saw a baby drop from its mother's arms as she staggered for a moment and fell over its body. He saw an old woman on the top of a wagon pitch forward and roll off into the road, where she lay still. He saw a young girl neatly dressed—she had been standing within a yard of him, staring up at the German plane—fall over a sleeping man and lie across his body until he sat up with a jerk and pushed her away. All that passed before Edward's eyes and entered his soul and burnt it with an unforgettable memory in just one second or two. During that second or two there had been no noise or panic in the crowd of refugees. Now they began screaming and running. Old men raised their fists to the sky and cursed the human being up there with black wings beneath him, now hardly visible beyond them as he flew farther towards Paris.

"Assassin! Bandit! . . . Foul pig! . . . Murderer of children!"

Edward regained the movement of his limbs and mind. He ran towards the girl who had fallen across the body of the sleeping man and stooped down and lifted her up a little in his arms. His hands were wet with her blood. She lay limp and heavy in his arms.

"Dead," said the man, who had been sleeping. "I woke up to find her dead across my legs. I was astonished."

A white-haired man came from behind a cart and put an arm across his eyes after staring at the girl, whom Edward now laid upon the grass as gently as he could. She lay with her face upwards to the blue sky, with her eyes open. Tall buttercups touched her white cheeks. Other men and women came to stand round her, crying out words of pity and horror.

A tall, grey-haired woman, dressed in black, went over to the man, who had covered his eyes with his arm, and put a thin brown hand on his shoulder and spoke to him.

"She is perhaps better dead, Jean. She has been spared many things."

The white-haired man dropped his arm and turned towards the woman and put his forehead against her thin breast and wept.

Chas Hunt came back to Edward. His eyes seemed on fire with a blazing anger.

"That son of Satan!" he said. "That deliberate murderer of women and children. I shall never forget this. I shall make a song of hate about it."

The French lieutenant, Armand de Rollencourt, came to speak to Edward, whom he seemed to regard as the man who had hired the taxi-cab.

"Is it possible," he asked politely, "that you should give a lift to a demoiselle who cannot walk any farther? She feels faint and ill. She happens to be a cousin of mine."

Edward glanced at Chas Hunt and asked: "Why not?"

"With pleasure," said Hunt to the lieutenant.

The young officer said: "A thousand thanks," and added a few words on his own behalf. "If you could take me back as far as my men . . ."

"That's understood," answered Hunt.

The taxi-driver came up and spoke in a trembling voice, and his hand quivered like a man who had been shell-shocked.

"This is a world of devils. God, if there is any God, has forsaken France."

"Are you hurt, old man?" asked Hunt.

"I am unhurt," said the man. "It is only my heart that bleeds. It is for my little Louise. She lies dead in her mother's arms. She was shot by that assassin of the sky. My poor Odette, whom I found by a miracle, weeps for her little one."

Hambledon did not speak at that moment. He was thinking about this scene and what it meant.

"This is total war," he thought. "That man is right. The devil has been let loose on France. These Nazis are without mercy and without pity. They have been educated in brutality and all cruelty. If they win it will be a hell on earth. And they are winning. Nothing can stop them. The German Devil is victorious. Where, then, is the God of whom this taxi-driver speaks? Perhaps it's a fairy-tale."

He looked about him and saw the sweet and lovely countryside, with green meadows through which a little river wandered with willows overhanging its banks, and wild flowers gleaming gold and silver in the tall grass by the roadside. Was this also a fairy-tale—an illusion of beauty? Anyhow, it was all spoilt by what had happened and what was going to happen. The refugees were on the move again. The farmcarts with their creaking wheels raised the white dust again as the old horses paced forward. The dead girl in the grass had been carried away and put into one of the carts. The dead babies had been put with the baggage and the bundles, or lay on the laps of the weeping mothers.

VIII

ONE OF THEM did not weep. It was Odette, the driver's daughter. She came, carrying her dead child clasped to her breast. Her dark eyes were deep set in a white face. Edward never forgot the look in those eyes. The Madonna might have looked like that when she stood before the Cross.

He sat opposite this girl and her dead baby for many kilometres along the roads of France. Armand de Rollencourt sat in front, next to the driver. The girl called Madeleine was next to Odette and presently fell asleep with her head on the other girl's shoulder. Chas Hunt and Edward were on the two turn-up seats with their backs to the driver.

"This is certainly going to be a slow business," said Hunt. "Unless we can escape down a side road we shan't get back tonight."

Edward nodded and said: "I guess that's so."

It was a long journey back. The Paris taxi-cab was trapped in the column of refugees and had to keep to the pace of the old farm-horses for a long distance. Every now and then the refugees halted for a rest of fifteen minutes or so. Owing to the heat of the afternoon and the dust they raised, they became parched with thirst, and many lay down in the grass of wayside meadows to drink from the little meandering stream, making cups of their hands.

Edward followed their example and washed his hands in the stream. He had wiped them on his handkerchief, but they were still stained with the blood of a dead girl.

No other black demon of the sky came to harry them and there was no noise about them but the creaking of cart-wheels and the quiet thud of horses' hoofs, and the twitter of birds in the bushes.

They did not talk to each other, these fugitives from terror. They were silent. It was a silence of physical weariness and agony of mind.

Not much was said inside the cab.

Once Chas Hunt spoke to Edward. "We must try to get down a side road. I don't care to spend the night in this cab."

For several kilometres there was no side road.

One of the halts was near the turn of the road where the two Americans had met the young lieutenant. He jumped down from his seat next to the driver and climbed on to the bank above the road. Edward watched him standing there motionless for a long minute. He came back and spoke through the open window.

"My men have gone. They have left the gun. They are deserters and cowards. It is this cowardice which dooms us to defeat."

He spoke with extreme bitterness and anger.

"Perhaps it was suicide to stay," said Hunt.

The girl called Madeleine had awakened. Edward saw her sit up and look at him with a kind of puzzled surprise as though wondering how she found herself in this cab with a stranger. Then she straightened herself up and wiped the dust off her lips with a tiny handkerchief. She had finely-cut features and brown eyes with long lashes like the etching of a girl's head by Helleu. She spoke for the first time.

"What are you going to do, Armand? Where are we going in this cab?"

The lieutenant stared at her as though he was utterly uncertain.

"What can I do?" he asked. "What can any of us do?"

He was silent for a moment and then spoke again.

"We are all refugees. I am a lieutenant in the French Army which is in retreat. God alone knows how far they have retreated. It is perhaps best to get back to Paris. Someone there may tell me where to go."

"I doubt it," said Hunt. "Paris is abandoned by all the Ministries. You will have to go as far as Bordeaux, *mon lieutenant*."

"Bordeaux!" echoed Armand de Rollencourt. "It is a long march from here." He gave a little, quiet, bitter laugh.

"What about me?" asked Madeleine. "Papa and Mamma may have left Paris."

She looked across at Edward. "What do you think, *M'sieur?* Is Paris quite deserted?"

Hambledon smiled at her.

"There are perhaps a million people left in Paris, but everybody is leaving who can leave. People with cars or people with a little money to keep them alive."

"What then shall I do if my parents have gone?" asked the girl.

"It is necessary to find out," said the lieutenant. "I am in the same situation, Madeleine. My father may still be at the château. He was very obstinate in his wish to stay there. I do not know whether my mother and sisters have gone. I know nothing."

He turned to Hambledon and Hunt and hesitated before speaking. Hunt guessed his thought. "We'll drop you at your château," he said. "How many kilometres from here?"

"Fifteen," answered the lieutenant. "It would be a great relief to me to find my parents, or to know if they have gone."

Hunt changed places with him and took the seat next to the driver. This time there was a long halt before the column moved again.

The lieutenant gave a groan. "We stay here all night!" he exclaimed.

The sun was beginning to sink below a line of tall poplars. The trees were black against bars of crimson and gold. Up above in the blue there were flame-tipped feathers.

Odette spoke to Edward. All this time she had sat quite silent, nursing her dead baby, so motionless and so white that she might have been dead also.

"I wish to speak to my father."

Hambledon turned sideways and told the taxi-driver. He got off his seat and opened the door of his cab.

"What is it, my poor Odette?"

"It is time to bury my baby This place is as good as any other, if there is time."

"It would be best," agreed the father. "Certainly it would be best to bury the child. I will make a little grave."

"Let me help you," said Edward.

He got out of the cab and held Odette's arm as she stepped down, still clasping the dead baby.

The others followed her.

The taxi-driver went over to one of the farmcarts and in a few moments came back with a spade.

"I will dig the grave," said Edward. "Your daughter needs you."

"A thousand thanks, *m'sieur*," said the taxi-driver.

Hambledon walked a little distance from the road and chose a spot close to a silver birch whose fresh leaves were like little green flames. His thoughts were busy as he dug a hole after cutting through the long grass.

"Good God!" he thought, "this is like a fantastic dream. Perhaps I am dreaming that I am digging a grave for a dead baby in France, killed out of the blue by a German machine-gun bullet. It's darned unreal. The odd thing is that I don't feel any emotion. I ought to have a sense of horror, but I haven't. I only have a sense of pity for that young mother, and a dull sort of astonishment that life should be like this. It's war against civilians. Bloody murder out of a blue sky against women and babies. Death in the sunshine with birds singing in the bushes and exquisite beauty in these fields of France. Here am I digging a grave—an American from Massachusetts digging a grave in a French meadow with hundreds of refugees watching me. Just a dream, maybe, like most other things in life. I wonder if this hole is deep enough."

Such thoughts passed through his head as he drove his spade into the earth. Drops of sweat trickled down his face and he wiped them away with the back of his hand.

"A thousand thanks *m'sieur*," said the taxi-driver again. "Come, Odette. Let me take the little one."

"I will do it," said the girl.

She kneeled down and laid the child in the grave as though putting it to bed, very tenderly.

Some of the women who had gathered near began to weep. An old man raised his fist to the sky and cursed the Germans. Odette did not weep when Edward took his spade again and put earth over the little body until the hole was filled up. Then suddenly she gave a cry and fell into her father's arms, weeping bitterly. A number of women closed round her, crying out words of comfort and pity.

Edward looked down at his work and then walked away for a few yards and picked some wild flowers in the long grass and came back to the little grave and laid them on it.

"Nicely done, Hambledon," said Chas Hunt, standing behind him.

They went back to the car. The column began to move again.

IX

IT WAS LATE and dark when the taxi-cab stopped outside an old gateway with wrought-iron gates between two stone pillars surmounted by heraldic griffins, just visible in the pale luminance of a clear sky in which a crescent moon was rising.

Odette's father had tried to escape from the main column of refugees by turning into a side road, but this was also choked by farmcarts and every kind of vehicle crawling down a narrower road. Now at last the taxi-cab had reached the château where the French lieutenant thought he might find his people.

He sprang down and opened the iron gates and then came back to speak through the window of the cab.

"Whatever happens," he said, "we must all spend the night here. It is impossible to get as far as Paris during the hours of darkness."

"That is true," agreed the taxi-driver, "and my daughter needs a rest."

"I guess we all need a rest," said Chas Hunt, whose bones were aching. Madeleine had sat for a long time with her arm round Odette, whose head was on her shoulder. She, too, must have felt cramped and aching.

"The house is half a mile up the drive," said Armand. "Drive carefully, for there is a ditch on one side."

They drove without lights, but the luminance of the sky was enough to give a whiteness to the winding road bordered by tall poplars. The faint light revealed the outlines of the château at the end of the drive, with its mansard roof and dormer windows flanked by two small towers with pointed turrets. It was a small château and looked old.

Lieutenant Armand de Rollencourt sprang up the steps and tugged at an iron bed-handle. The clanging of a bell inside sounded through the silence. There was no answer to that summons.

Edward and his fellow travellers had followed the lieutenant up the steps.

"They have gone," he said. "Undoubtedly, my father must have decided to go with the others."

He pushed against the oak door at the top of the steps and found it was unlocked and a little ajar.

"Well, we can get in," he said. "That is something. When you have come in, I will turn up the lights."

He shut the door after them when they stepped into the darkness of a hall which lighted up when he touched a switch. The floor was stone-flagged, and on one side was a big open fireplace below a heavily carved chimney-piece. Round the walls, below a high-timbered roof with black cross-beams, were the heads of stags and boars and other hunting trophies, mangy and dust covered. The room was littered with papers and card-board boxes. On a wooden settle by the fireplace was a leather trunk half filled with women's clothes, which spilt over to the floor where a silk frock lay under two high-heeled shoes. A wooden packing-case stood in the centre of the hall stuffed with other clothes shoved in untidily.

"They have left in a hurry," said the lieutenant. "They have had to leave many things behind. No doubt they have gone to our farm."

He strode further down the hall and switched on more light. At the far end was a broad staircase with heavily carved banisters. He went up a few stairs and shouted out, as though not quite sure that the house was deserted in spite of his last words.

"Papa! . . . Maman! . . . Lucile! . . . Marie-Louise! . . . Pierre! . . ."

He turned and spoke to his guests.

"This is an empty château. We are alone here."

He went upstairs to a gallery from which several rooms opened. Most of the doors were open and he went inside, turning up lights, and then, after a glance, switching them out again. In one room he stayed for a few minutes and came out carrying some papers. Perhaps he had been into his own bedroom.

"Pardon me," he said, coming downstairs. "You are all hungry. I must try to find you some food. If you will come into the salon. . . ."

He opened a door from the hall and lighted up a big room furnished as a drawing-room, stiffly, in the French style with gilt-backed chairs, and Empire writing-tables and couches. On the walls were some modern portraits—one of this young lieutenant in his uniform, looking very gallant and debonair.

"Perhaps one of you gentlemen would come and forage with me," he suggested.

He looked at Edward, who followed him down a narrow passage leading out of the hall to an immense kitchen with larders and pantries beyond.

"This is an interesting old château," said Edward. "It looks quite ancient."

"Partly of the sixteenth century," answered the young lieutenant. "My father has spent a lot of money on it. My sister and I are devoted to it. We were brought up here as children. We have played hide-and-seek in all its rooms. Our beautiful mother also adores this place though it is very rustic and shabby. For me it is haunted by the spirit of our youth . . . in days of happiness—before this atrocious war."

He was silent for a moment and then gave a slight groan.

"Now all that is past. In a few days . . . or a few hours . . . the Germans will be here. They will ransack the house. They will turn over my mother's clothes and private letters and family photographs. They will kick my father's books about. They will swill beer in this kitchen, and lie with their muddy boots on beds and sofas. In the winter they will tear down the panelling to make fires. They will behave like brutes and barbarians in this old château of France where I first saw the light of day."

He spoke with extreme bitterness which amounted to mental agony.

"All very lamentable," said Edward. "*Effroyable.*"

Armand de Rollencourt nodded and spoke more calmly.

"It is the fate of France which I think about most. One could bear one's personal losses, but what is going to happen to France? I cannot think. I dare not think. It is too frightful. But why do I talk so much while you are hungry? I am lacking in hospitality. I forget my manners."

He went into a larder and peered about and then gave a little cry.

"A leg of mutton! Some cold potatoes! That is something. If I could find some bread and perhaps a bottle of wine. . . ."

There was no bread, but he found a tin of biscuits and two bottles of wine, heavily cobwebbed, which he brought from the cellars.

Edward carried them into the salon, and presently the lieutenant followed with some knives and forks and a pile of plates upon which Edward noticed a family crest. It was the griffin which surmounted the two stone pillars at the gate.

"You must be famished, Madeleine," said Armand to the girl with brown eyes and long lashes. As Edward knew afterwards, she was Madeleine Delaroche and a cousin of Armand.

"I am as hungry as a starved dog," she said with a smile. "One must eat, whatever happens."

"Where is our taxi-driver and his daughter?" asked Armand, glancing round.

"I put Odette to bed," answered Madeleine Delaroche. "In the little room where I used to sleep. Her father is sitting by her side holding her hand. She is very unwell."

"Poor creature!" said Armand.

They had a picnic meal in the salon with its gilt-backed chairs. Armand poured out the wine, having fetched more glasses. It was good French Burgundy—*Moulin-a-Vent*.

Madeleine Delaroche raised her glass and spoke in a low voice.

"*Vive la France!*"

"Our poor France!" answered Armand with a faint groan.

Edward sipped his wine in honour of this toast. In spite of defeat France would live. Not Hitler nor all his legions could kill the soul of France. He had read French poetry. He was steeped in its spirit. He loved the French people, though he knew the corruption of their politicians and the little meannesses of the *bourgeoisie*.

After they had eaten Armand went out of the salon. Madeleine spoke to Edward and Chas Hunt.

"My cousin Armand is very charming. Do you not agree?"

They agreed.

"His father was a General in the last war," she told them. "He is a very noble old man and a great patriot. He is too old to have command in this war, alas! He will be broken-hearted by all this tragedy of defeat."

She looked at Edward and asked a question as she leaned forward in her chair with one arm on her knee and her little chin cupped in her hand.

"Do you think we are near the end? Do you think we shall have to surrender to those devils? I would not dare ask Armand."

Even Edward was shocked by that word surrender. His thoughts had not travelled as far as that. He could not bring himself to believe that France would raise the White Flag.

"That is a terrible idea, *mademoiselle*," he answered. "I hope that will not happen."

"Those old men, Weygand and Pétain," said Madeleine Delaroche. "They are, I think, *gaga*. They did not prepare for this war. The President Lebrun slept and did nothing. Many of our Generals were politicians and Fascists. They ignored General de Gaulle, who wrote a book on mechanized warfare. They have given him only a subordinate command. We are very weak in the tanks and armoured cars which he advocated so strongly. Our air force is almost negligible compared with the enemy's."

She was a pretty girl of twenty or so, in a short frock which showed her knees when she sat. It was strange to hear such words from her lips. Chas Hunt seemed to think so. He smiled at her before he answered.

"What you say is, I am afraid, very true, *mademoiselle*. But how do you know these things? You speak like a military expert."

She smiled back at him with a flutter of her long lashes.

"Perhaps I speak like a parrot. My father is a Colonel, now retired. He was for a time military critic for *Le Temps*. I have read his articles. I have listened to his long tirades—which I thought very tiresome and coloured by his prejudice. Now, alas, I know they were true."

She accepted a cigarette which Chas Hunt offered her from his case. After putting Odette to bed upstairs she had washed the white dust from her face and hands and arms, and brushed her brown hair. She had more than a touch of elegance and grace and looked at home in this salon of a château in France.

"What is that?" she asked suddenly. "It is a queer noise."

Edward had heard that queer noise. It sounded to him like the strangled cry of a man in some fear or agony. He rose from his chair and walked across the hall. He had an idea that the cry came from Armand de Rollencourt and from a room across the hall on the other side of the salon.

Its door was shut, but Edward opened it and saw Armand in a book-lined room with heavy curtains over the windows and a tiger-skin rug on the floor. The lieutenant was standing motionless with his back to the door. He was staring at something on the floor near a big writing-desk. It was the body of an old man in a General's uniform with many decorations. He lay crumpled up sideways with one arm sprawled across the tiger skin, which was stained by a patch of blackish red.

Suddenly the lieutenant gave a hard sob and went down on his knees and kissed the forehead of the old man and wept.

Hambledon bent down and put his hand on the lieutenant's shoulder.

"I'm sorry," he said. "Shall I go?"

"Don't go," answered Armand. "I beg of you not to go."

He stood up again, grasping Edward's arm.

"My father has shot himself. He put on his old uniform and all the decorations he had won in the last war. He could not bear the thought that France should be vanquished—after all the sacrifice of the last war—after the victory which he helped to gain last time. He stayed behind to kill himself. He preferred death."

He turned and spoke sharply, in a low voice.

"Shut that door. Do not let the others come in. Stay with me a little while, my friend."

Hambledon shut the door and turned the key and stood while a lieutenant of France went down on his knees again by his dead father.

It was a fantastic night in the château de Rollencourt. Edward Hambledon looked back upon it sometimes as a nightmare of war which he had dreamed in another life.

Chas Hunt was all for pushing on to Paris. He was anxious to send a dispatch to his New York paper, perhaps the last he would be able to send before Paris was occupied by the enemy, but this idea was made impossible when the taxi-driver came downstairs with the news that Odette was very sick and in no state to continue the journey.

"In any case," he said, "it is mad to try and reach Paris by night. The refugees will be camped on the roads. We couldn't go a kilometre from here without getting stuck. My poor Odette may feel stronger in the morning."

Chas Hunt said "Hell!" under his breath to Edward.

Madeleine Delaroche went upstairs to look after Odette, and Armand, who had come out of his father's study, gave another reason for not leaving the château that night.

"I must bury my father. I cannot leave him without burial until the Germans come. It would be a dishonour."

Edward had a secret and startling thought.

"Have I become the grave-digger of France—the second time today?"

He was relieved when Armand turned to the taxi-driver and spoke a few words to him.

"You will help me dig my father's grave? Is that asking too much, my friend?"

"At your service, *mon lieutenant*," answered the man, whose name was now known to them as Jean Meudon.

"Gentlemen," said Armand, addressing the two Americans, "this is a tragic affair. I deeply regret to ask your aid in such a painful episode. But my father is a heavy man. Perhaps you would be good enough to help carry him when I and our friend here have dug a grave in the park?"

"You can count on us, lieutenant," said Hunt.

It was a strange scene in the moonlight by the open grave which, an hour later, had been dug by Armand de Rollencourt and Jean Meudon.

Hambledon and Hunt helped to carry out the General's body wrapped in the tiger-skin rug. Certainly he was a heavy man and Hambledon found himself breathing hard by the time he reached the grave.

"Let us take a rest for a moment," said Armand. "Then we will lower him."

A slim figure came out of the darkness by the château. It was Madeleine Delaroche, who came to stand by the grave of her uncle.

"Now, gentlemen," said Armand.

As they laid the General in his last resting-place the earth shook. Somewhere not far away there were heavy explosions and suddenly flames leapt into the sky, followed by clouds of smoke which became rosy in the light of the flames.

"They are bombing Pontoise, or thereabouts," said Armand in a low voice.

"It is not amusing," said Madeleine Delaroche.

She clutched Edward's arm.

"It's all right," he said, reassuringly.

"It will frighten my daughter," said Jean Meudon. "We had better hurry up this business."

He began to throw the earth into the grave.

Armand stood still and made the sign of the Cross on his forehead and breast. He had put a lantern by the edge of the grave, and its glimmer of light sparkled on the buttons of his tunic.

Hunt spoke in English to Hambledon, when they stepped back a few paces by some bushes waiting for Armand de Rollencourt, by whose side Madeleine now stood, weeping silently.

"I'm not darned sure that this isn't a dream, Hambledon."

"I'll say it's dream-like," answered Edward. "But it's a bad dream, Chas."

"I'm getting nervous about being away from Paris so long," said Hunt, still speaking in a low voice. "I'll be in Queer Street with my paper if I'm not there when the Germans walk in."

It was Hambledon who was first startled by a movement in the bushes behind him. It was like an animal moving there. He swung round and saw something dark coming out of the bushes. It was a man wearing a blue béret over a blue shirt tucked into corduroy trousers. He was powdered from head to foot in the white dust of the roads. He spoke in a hoarse whisper.

"Are you English?"

"American," answered Edward, whispering back because of Armand and Madeleine standing by the grave. "Who are you?"

"My name is Hardy. I was taken prisoner near Dieppe. I gave them the slip. I'm a captain in the Rifle Brigade."

"How did you get here?" asked Hambledon.

"I've been walking with the refugees. My leg gave out. I was wounded by a machine-gun bullet and it's not too good."

"Better get into the château," whispered Edward. "We can't talk here."

"No, I'm sorry," said the English officer. "Do you mind if I grab your arm?"

He gripped Hambledon's arm and walked painfully towards the château.

"I don't know if I can make those steps," he said, fifty paces farther on.

"We'll help you," said Hunt.

The two Americans put their arms round the wounded man and carried him up the steps, and then into the house and into the salon, where they laid him down on a couch.

"This is marvellous!" said the English officer, looking round the room. "Very civilized. Very charming. After Dieppe. . . ." He gave a faint laugh as though amused by a fantastic contrast.

He was a man under thirty, perhaps, with a clean-cut English face and blue eyes which did not go well with his disguise as a French peasant.

"How did you get those clothes, captain?" asked Hambledon.

"From one of the refugees. He undid his bundle and I changed behind a hedge. He was a grand fellow. I take back all my prejudice against the French after walking with those refugees until this leg of mine gave me hell."

Armand de Rollencourt came into the salon with Madeleine and was astonished to see a man dressed as a peasant on his Empire couch talking English to the two Americans.

"Who is this?" he asked.

Captain Hardy tried to rise, but it was too painful. It was Hambledon who introduced them.

"An escaped English Captain, *mon lieutenant*. Badly wounded near Dieppe."

De Rollencourt prevented him from standing up and was excited to meet an escaped officer of the British Army.

"It is an honour to have you here," he said. "I hope your wound is not too painful."

He spoke other words very courteously.

"First of all I must bring you some refreshment, *mon capitaine*. A thousand pardons for not thinking of that immediately. After that we will attend to your wound."

"It is very good of you, sir," answered Captain Christopher Hardy in excellent French. "But I'm sorry to give you any trouble. You have had enough already."

"You have been fighting for France," answered the lieutenant. "You are one of our comrades."

While Captain Hardy was eating the last meat on a leg of mutton and drinking a glass of French Burgundy something happened which startled them all. Madeleine Delaroche had just poured out a second glass of wine for the wounded officer when everything in the room shook and trembled. Some cut-glass candelabra tinkled, and a vase on the carved chimney-piece fell off and smashed to bits. Hambledon felt his chair shaking beneath him and the white panelled walls of the salon creaked and all the room vibrated.

"*O mon Dieu!*" exclaimed Armand, rising from his chair and listening intently. He listened, as they all listened, to a grinding, crunching, lumbering sound of heavy machines moving up the avenue of the park and shaking the earth.

It was Captain Hardy who knew the meaning of it first.

"German tanks."

He rose from the couch, holding on to its back. "What are we going to do about it?" he asked. "Is there anywhere to hide? I should hate to be taken prisoner again."

A very bright light came into the room through the shuttered windows. It was as though a searchlight had been turned upon them.

Armand thought quickly.

"They will have seen our lights. There must be somebody here when they come. Madeleine?"

Her face was dead white, but she answered quietly, "I will stay, Armand."

"These two American gentlemen," said Armand. "They are not in danger, perhaps."

"That's all right with us," said Hambledon.

"The captain and I will hide ourselves," said Armand. "They may not stay long. There are some good cellars here, *mon capitaine*. I regret your wound will give you pain. Take my arm."

There was a louder sound of grinding machines and the scrunch of heavy monsters nearer to the château. A harsh voice rasped out, clearly audible. "*Achtung! Geh' herum!*"

"*Mon Dieu!*" said Madeleine in a fainting whisper.

Armand's face blenched at the sound of German.

"The horror has arrived," he said in a low voice.

He turned quickly to the two Americans and held out his hand to Edward.

"I thank you," he said. "I shall never forget your kindness in these painful hours."

"We shall meet again," said Hambledon. "Before the end comes we Americans will be fighting in France."

It was an astonishing thing to say then. The words slipped from him without thought, but he remembered them afterwards and wondered at his own prophecy when the Germans were driving towards Paris, when the British were standing on Dunkirk sands, when England stood alone against Hitler with all his power. It was as though he had seen something far in the future of this war, and got ahead of time.

Armand went quickly to Madeleine, his cousin, and held her for a moment in his arms and kissed her. Then he bent down and helped Captain Hardy to get up.

"Put your arm round my shoulder," he said. Very slowly and painfully Hardy walked out of the room with this aid, and those three who were left heard his dragging steps.

Someone had tugged at the iron chain outside which rang the big bell in the hall. It rang noisily, with its iron tongue striking the bronze with deep resonance.

"I'll go," said Hambledon.

He saw Madeleine standing there in the salon with a face of dead whiteness. Hunt was also standing and looked uneasy.

Edward Hambledon did not feel at ease during those moments when he strode across the hall floor to open the big oak door. He could feel that his heart was thumping. It was not with any fear exactly, though it was on the cards that a German thug might shoot the man who opened the door to them, but there was something very sinister in this summons by the enemy. It was a moment of high drama which had a tense effect upon him.

The bell clanged again impatiently and was still reverberating when Hambledon pulled back a chain and bolt and opened the door, letting a floor of light into the darkness of the drive and its open space in front of the château. He had a moment's glimpse of German tanks, perhaps twenty, in a mass of metal below the steps. Men were jumping down from them—grim-looking robots in steel helmets low on the neck. Immediately in front of him on the flagged terrace above the steps were half a dozen figures. One of them spoke in French.

"We regret to disturb you at this time of night, but we wish to stay here before we go further towards Paris. You will doubtless excuse us."

It was the voice of a young man and he spoke good French, though with the heavy German r, and seemed remarkably polite.

Hambledon saw that he was the tallest of these figures who stood outside the door.

"I am not the owner of this château," answered Hambledon. "The family is away except for one young lady, who is a relative."

"*Très bien*," answered the tall young man. "Then our visit will not be alarming. In any case, there is no cause for alarm. We are, I hope, civilized."

"I hope so," answered Edward, dryly.

His heart had ceased thumping. He felt that the tension had slackened.

Some of the other figures on the step began to speak in German. Two of them thrust past Edward and entered the hall. The others stopped talking when the tallest among them rasped out some commands to the men below the terrace who had jumped out of their tanks. Then he turned to Edward and spoke in French again.

"We are a little fatigued. The heat and dust of the roads is terrible. It will be pleasant to have a short respite in this old château of France which looks quite romantic."

He entered the hall, followed by the others who had waited for him, and took off his steel helmet. By the light of the hall Edward saw that he was a young man with short fair hair and a sunburnt face with deep-set blue eyes.

He gave a quick glance round the hall and smiled as he spoke.

"Very romantic! Certainly mediaeval. Once no doubt the home of French knights, and fair ladies like Marguerite de Valois."

Edward did not answer this romantic sentiment. He was aware that the other officers—they were certainly officers—were staring at him. Perhaps they saw that he was not French and may have suspected that he was English.

He had left the door of the salon open and the tall young man strode into it and then halted at the sight of Madeleine, who stood there with her dead white face. He clicked his heels and bowed to her stiffly and then spoke reassuring words.

"I regret this intrusion, *mademoiselle*. There is no cause for alarm. We wish to behave in the most correct way possible. Permit me to introduce myself. Graf Kurt von Eupen."

Madeleine Delaroche did not answer and did not move. She looked as though she stood there dead. For a moment Graf von Eupen looked at her with an uneasy smile as though embarrassed by this silence and lack of acknowledgment. Then he saw Hunt, and clicked his heels again and repeated his name.

Hunt nodded coldly.

"I am an American," he said.

The tall young German looked surprised, and answered, "An American? That is interesting. How do you come to be in this château?"

"We came here with this young lady, and a young mother who lies upstairs very ill because her child was killed by one of your airmen who fired on the refugees."

For a moment the young German looked disconcerted.

"That is regrettable," he said. "War is very terrible, is it not?"

"You make it against women and children," said Hunt harshly. "In Holland, in Poland. Now here in France."

Graf von Eupen raised his hands slightly.

"It is total war," he answered. "There is no distinction between soldiers and civilians. It is the most merciful way of making war because it ends more quickly. The losses are less in the long run."

"It is devilish," said Hunt, breathing hard and staring at this young German fiercely.

"We carry out the orders of our Führer," said the German officer. "Under his leadership this war will be a short one. Complete victory is within our reach and he will establish a new order in Europe."

He turned towards Edward politely.

"Are you also an American?" he asked.

"I am," answered Edward.

"Perhaps you will permit me to see your passports. As a matter of form."

He examined the passports carefully and handed them back.

"Perfectly in order."

The other German officers were examining the pictures on the walls and some china in the cabinets. They talked to each other quietly and seemed subdued by the elegance of this room in contrast to their own dust-powdered uniforms and greasy faces. They were young men, not much past boyhood, and one of them made a joke at which the others laughed.

"We should like to wash ourselves," said Graf von Eupen, addressing Edward. "Are there any facilities for that?"

Madeleine spoke for the first time. She did not look at the German officer but at Edward.

"There is a wash-place behind the kitchen. You will direct them, *m'sieur?*"

Hambledon showed them the way to the kitchen and to the wash-place beyond. Then he came back to the salon, from which he could hear gusts of laughter and guttural shouts from the German tank crews outside the château.

"This is a horrible experience," said Madeleine. "I nearly fainted when those men came in. What shall we do now? I am very anxious about Armand."

"We must prevent them from going down into the cellars," said Hambledon. "They may go and look for wine. That fellow von Eupen said they would be glad to drink some French wine.

"Better bring it up before they go down," said Hunt.

Madeleine volunteered to act as guide.

"I will help you find it. I will come down with you."

"We shall need a light," said Edward.

He lit two candles from a mantelshelf and gave one to Madeleine, in whose hand it wavered as she led the way to some stone stairs at the end of the hall. They were very close to the German officers in the wash-room. They could hear them talking and laughing. There was the splash of water in the basins and one of them was singing.

Edward stumbled for a moment on the stone steps leading down to the cellars and Madeleine whispered an exclamation of fear.

Hunt followed by the light of their candles, which seemed lost in the darkness when they went further down.

It was cold and dark down there in the cellar and there was a smell of dampness and mildew.

"We shall need a dozen bottles at least," said Hambledon. He found the wine bins and took out the bottles. It was Burgundy of an old vintage by the feel of the cobwebs round them.

Madeleine called out in a low voice, "Armand! . . . Armand! . . ."

A door creaked and opened an inch and then wider. Armand de Rollencourt came through the door.

"What has happened?" he asked. "Why have you come down here?"

It was Madeleine who explained in a whispered conversation.

"I must get out of uniform," said Armand presently. "Madeleine, you will find some old suits of mine in the wardrobe in my room upstairs. Bring me down the oldest you can find."

"Where is the English captain?" asked Hunt.

Armand pointed to the other door.

"I've hidden him under some straw. His leg hurts him horribly, I fear."

"I will go up with the wine," said Hambledon.

"Come on, Hunt. We must get some glasses."

They reached the salon again before the officers had finished washing, but only a second or two before.

They came striding across the hall in their heavy boots and entered the salon when the two Americans were arranging the glasses on one of the tables. They looked younger and fresher now that they had cleaned themselves up. It was Graf von Eupen who first saw the bottles of wine.

"This is admirable," he said. "A thousand thanks."

He turned and spoke in German to his brother officers, who laughed. Some of them sat down on the gilt-backed chairs and lit cigars and cigarettes.

"We will leave you now," said Edward. "My friend and I will get some sleep."

"By all means," answered the Panzer officer. "We will try not to disturb you."

But it was three hours past midnight before there was any quietude in the salon. Edward Hambledon, sitting on a chest in a bedroom upstairs, listened to their laughter and noise. Every now and then they sang German soldier songs, harmonizing them rather well. One of them kept making a speech, interrupted by loud laughter and shouts. Once a table crashed over and there was a sound of breaking glass. Some of them were getting drunk on good French wine. The salon door opened now and then and one of the German officers strode across the hall to the wash-place, his heavy boots thumping across the stone-flagged floor. A reek of cigars came up to the bedrooms.

In a room near to the one where Edward sat listening intently there was the sound of a woman weeping incessantly.

Edward sat in darkness except for a glimmer through the windows. Once there was a tap at the door which startled him.

"Who is there?" he asked sharply.

He thought it might be one of those drunken boys searching for a bed. But it was Madeleine Delaroche. She stood inside his door, shading a candle with her hand.

"I want to get some clothes for Armand," she said.

Through the open door, which afterwards she closed very quietly, there came the sound of that weeping, mingled with the laughter and singing of the Germans downstairs.

"Odette weeps her heart out for the dead child," said Madeleine.

With Edward's help she found a suit of clothes for Armand and one of his shirts.

"If I meet one of those *Boches*," she said, "it will be abominable. He will want to know why I am carrying a civilian suit. I must creep down while they are still drinking."

She crept down presently. Hambledon stood at his door watching and listening. He saw her puff out the candle beginning to light up the hall which she crossed like a ghost. Suddenly one of the Germans left the salon again. Madeleine was standing motionless in the darkness at the top of the cellar steps.

In the next room Odette was moaning.

Dawn came with the first gleam of light through the bedroom windows. It was the end of a strange night in the life of an American.

X

EDWARD HAMBLEDON DID some thinking in that bedroom before and after the approach of dawn. Parts of this thinking went across the Atlantic to his home in Massachusetts. They would be wondering what was happening to him—his father and mother, and his sister Penny (short for Penelope) and his brother Tiny, so called because he stood six-foot-two in his socks. Edward hadn't written for nearly a couple of months, being a bad letter-writer, but he had had a cable from his father saying: "Better come home." Penny's last scrawl, written in a train, had told him that the family had gone back to Lakeside Farm after the winter in Boston. She was looking forward to some riding again and heaps of bathing. Mother was busy, as usual, with lots of committees, and had been attending a course of lectures on the philosophy of Rudolf Steiner, which seemed to give her much inward satisfaction, though Penny herself couldn't make head or tail of it. Father was worrying over the world situation which he didn't seem to like, and they were all shocked by the horrors in Poland and Holland. Tiny had announced at breakfast that he was a complete pacifist and isolationist, and she had pulled his hair at talking such nonsense so early in the morning. The Arkwrights were giving a dance for Susan's twenty-first birthday. The silver birches in the woods round Lakeside Farm were clothed in green again. The men were mowing the golf-course, which looked fine. In a postscript she added casually that she had become engaged, but not very seriously, to Spike Brandon.

That letter in a girl's scrawl had come into his mind in Armand de Rollencourt's bedroom while a young mother was weeping and moaning in a room near by, and when German officers were drinking downstairs and singing old soldier songs in a château of France.

The silver birches. . . . It was curious that his mind should travel as far as those woods with bare rocks jutting out of the soil by Assawampsett Lake three thousand miles away from this bedroom. His father had bought the place for a wad of dollars when they were kids. They had had a grand time there, growing up, and having great adventures during holidays from the town house in Boston. Afterwards at Harvard he had been a half-baked intellectual writing bad poetry, a devotee of T. S. Eliot and other modernists. He had fallen in love with beauty and made a religion of it. He had been scornful of the vulgar herd, as he called the ordinary folk about him. He had hated ugliness, and cruelty, and dollar-hunters, and loud-mouthed politicians, and patriotic boloney. He had abhorred the idea of war and had been all for Chamberlain's policy of appeasement and his trips to Munich. Funny, all that! Now he had been caught up in the tide of World War II. He had dug a grave for a little French corpse. He had stood by the graveside of a French General buried in his own park. Downstairs were German officers getting drunk. A bit of a contrast to family life in Massachusetts and peace in the U.S.A.!

His mind jerked back from this day-dream to the realities of his present situation. He was mixed up with a strange bunch of refugees from terror. He admired the spirit of that girl Madeleine. She had almost killed that German officer by the look in her eyes. That wounded Englishman was a good type, with charming manners and a good humour in spite of pain. Armand de Rollencourt was also a good type in his own line, but without the English sense of humour. Anyhow, he couldn't be humorous with Germans in his family château and his father not yet cold in his grave.

Then there was Jean Meudon, the taxi-driver, and that poor girl Odette. He couldn't let them down. He would have to see them through this episode, and help to find a way of escape for them. That wouldn't be easy as far as Armand and the English captain were concerned.

Hunt came into his room when dawn was breaking. He had found a bed elsewhere but said he hadn't slept a wink.

"What's the set-up downstairs?" asked Hambledon.

"The Germans are asleep," answered Hunt. "We had better get busy before they wake up."

Edward nodded.

"That's my idea. What about the French lieutenant and the English captain? Do you think they can make a get-away?"

This question was answered by Armand de Rollencourt. He came into the room stealthily and closed the door with careful quietude.

"Gentlemen," he said, "there is no time to waste. We must get away now. It is, at least, necessary for me and the English officer who is an escaped prisoner of war. Our only chance is dependent upon your kindness again. If you will take us as far as Paris in your taxi-cab. . . ."

It was impossible to take them as far as Paris in the taxi-cab. That was made plain by Jean Meudon when he came down into the cellar, where a rendezvous had been arranged.

"We are completely in the basket," he said gruffly. "These swine have taken my petrol. I have just met one of the German 'non.-coms.' He is up already and prowling about. When he saw me looking at my cab he laughed and said something in his barbarous speech which sounds like the gibbering of an ourang-outang. He laughed again when I swore at him and showed me his revolver. It was a hint which I did not ignore. For my poor Odette's sake I wish to keep alive."

Armand de Rollencourt was speechless for a moment. He raised his hands with a gesture of despair.

"That makes it very difficult."

Presently the wounded English officer staggered up from a pile of straw on which he had been lying.

"You must go without me," he said. "I'm a handicap. I will crawl into the woods and do the best I can."

"No, no," said Armand, hastily. "We are comrades. We will not abandon you, my friend."

"I doubt whether I can walk more than a few yards," said Captain Hardy. "You must look after yourselves. I hate making a nuisance of myself. In fact, I refuse to do so, and I'm an obstinate fellow!"

Armand shook his head.

"There is only one thing to do. We must join the crowd of refugees on the roads. We shall be lost among them. We will put you on one of their farmcarts. But we must get away before the *réveillé;* that is to say, before another half-hour has passed."

"There is already a German pig prowling about," he was reminded by Jean Meudon. "And the sentries are all round the tanks and at the gates."

"We will take a field path through the park," said Armand. "Jean Meudon, you will fetch your daughter. You agree to this plan, gentlemen?"

He looked at Hambledon and Hunt, who agreed. There was no other way than walking, now that the taxi-cab was out of action.

Jean Meudon was gloomy.

"I regret leaving my cab. It was a humiliation and an outrage. It belonged to me, this taxi-cab. It has been part of my life."

There were tears in his eyes. It was as though he were parting from a woman he loved.

"*C'est la guerre*," said Armand de Rollencourt, putting a hand on his shoulder for a moment.

In the pale light of dawn there was a strange little procession along a field path which led away from the Château de Rollencourt through its park. They had left the château by a back way through some outhouses and the dairy, and then across an open paddock screened by poplar trees. The four men—Armand and Jean Meudon, Hambledon and Hunt—took turns in carrying Captain Hardy on a hurdle which they used as a stretcher. Madeleine Delaroche walked with Odette, who looked desperately ill after her tragic night, but walked with courage.

A bugle rang out in the park. It was the *réveillé* to the German Panzer unit.

Birds were twittering in the bushes. The grass was wet with dew and spangled with the silver and gold of wild flowers. The sun was rising in a glory of pale gold.

Armand de Rollencourt looked back at the old château when he reached an iron gate leading on to a winding road.

"The house of my family!" he exclaimed in a tragic voice. "In the hands of the enemy!"

Hambledon tried to be of comfort.

"One day you will go back. Life always moves in circles."

"Not always," answered Armand. "There is death."

Half a mile down the road they came in touch with another column of refugees. They joined them and walked with them when Captain Hardy had been lifted on to one of the farmcarts, after some whispered words to a sturdy old man who owned it.

"An English officer. An escaped prisoner of war. You will take the risk?"

"Willingly. It is a question of honour, is it not?"

It was a long way to Paris.

XI

THIS WALK TO Paris was not amusing, but for Edward Hambledon an experience worth having, perhaps, because it brought him nearer to the French people in their suffering and in their courage. These old men and women, these young mothers and children—with a few young men among them who had not been called up for military service because they were producing food from the soil—were footsore and dirty, and apprehensive of the unknown future and the immediate present, but they were marvellously patient, on the whole, with a quiet resignation and fortitude.

Hambledon moved about among them, trying to be helpful to some of those who needed help.

"Hang on to my arm, madame," he said to an elderly woman who looked exhausted.

"My spirit is strong, but my old feet are weak," she told him.

"Can't you get a place on one of these farmcarts?" he asked her.

She shook her head.

"They are for the old women—poor old grandmothers—and for young mothers with their babes. One of them is my daughter. She has a child only three weeks old."

She spoke to him about the war.

"God asked too much of us. We suffered too much last time. My man was killed on the Somme in '17, and three of my brothers elsewhere. One of them at Souchez in '15. He was a young one. Another at Verdun, where so many died. Another on the Chemin des Dames."

She looked up at Hambledon while she clung to his arm.

"You are English?"

"American."

"American? You arrived late last time. Two years late."

"We came in at the end," answered Edward. "It will be the same this time."

"You will have to come in," said the elderly woman, who spoke in good French with only a touch of dialect. "This is a war against the Devil and his spirit of evil threatening the soul of humanity. The

Americans are against that, from what I have heard. They must come in one day."

They camped by the wayside several times a day and those who had brought food with them, on the carts or on wheelbarrows, or in bags strapped to their backs, shared it with others less provided. They shared it with Hambledon and his companions.

"A little wine, *M'sieur l'Americain?*" asked one old fellow. "It is not bad. It was in my cellar for the last ten years."

He poured out a mugful for Edward and held it out in his skinny hand.

"Drink to the death of Hitler," he said, with an old man's cackle of laughter. "That bandit. That assassin. That invader of other people's countries."

Edward took one sip and then, when the old man was not looking, carried it over to the cart where Captain Hardy was lying on a bundle of mattresses. Edward climbed on to one of the shafts and handed him the mug of wine.

"This will make you feel good," he said. "Strong peasant wine."

"Devilish good of you, old man," said Captain Hardy. "I'm as thirsty as a brick-kiln. Think I must have been a bit feverish. I found myself singing nursery rhymes. 'Three Blind Mice' and 'Here We Go Round the Mulberry Bush.' "

A young woman, sitting with her back to a wheel of the cart, spoke to Edward about him.

"Your English friend will get into trouble if the Germans catch up with us. He has been talking incessantly in his own tongue and singing funny little songs in a loud voice. They tell me he has escaped from the *Boches* after fighting in Dieppe. Is that true?"

"Quite true," answered Edward; "but not a story to tell everyone."

The girl laughed and shook her head.

"We shan't give him away. We are not friends of Herr Hitler. Come and sit down and eat some of this bread and ham. You look as if you need it."

Edward needed it. He was as hungry as a tiger, having had no breakfast. But he hated to take the food of these refugees.

"Can you spare a small piece," he asked. "It's very generous of you."

"No, it isn't generous," the girl contradicted him quickly. "We are not selfish pigs, you know. We are glad to share with our fellow-travellers. Perhaps there are some who hide their stuff. That's because of their fear of the future and because human nature is not angelic, especially among peasants."

Obviously she was not of peasant stock. She was neatly dressed in a black frock, cut low so that it showed her white neck round which was a string of sham pearls. She had been riding a bicycle which now lay on the grass close by.

"I was a schoolmistress in Dieppe," she told him. "I forget whether that was a month ago or a hundred years."

"I guess it wasn't a hundred years," answered Edward, munching a ham sandwich of considerable size and quality. "At least, you have not aged very much if it is as long as that."

She turned her head sideways and smiled at him.

"Thank you for the compliment, Mr. Englishman."

He did not trouble to tell her that he was an American.

"Where are you going now?" he asked. "What's your plan for the future?"

She raised both hands, long thin hands, as he noticed with an artist's eye.

"The future? That is all in darkness. Perhaps, in trying to escape, we are walking towards death. The Germans will swarm everywhere, like vermin, if France has to surrender."

"France hasn't surrendered yet," said Edward.

"We do not deceive ourselves," she told him. "Even these peasants do not deceive themselves. We know that our armies were betrayed, even before this war began. Not enough tanks, not enough aeroplanes, not enough anything. We cannot stand against the weight of Hitler's fury. Is not that the truth?"

"I'm afraid so."

"I go to Tours to find my mother and father," she told him. "From Paris it may still be possible to get to Tours. But unless I find my sister in Paris, which is unlikely, I shall not have enough money to go to Tours. That would create a serious situation."

She gave a little uneasy laugh at the prospect of this situation.

"Very unpleasant," agreed Edward.

Presently, after a further talk with her, he put his hand to his breast-pocket and drew out a black note-case.

"Would you allow me to give you the fare to Tours?" he asked. "In return for your ham sandwich, which was worth far more than that."

She looked at him sharply.

"Are you serious? Why should you give me this money?"

He answered her lightly.

"Just because I should hate you to get into that serious situation."

She looked displeased and suspicious.

"It is my affair," she told him. "Thank you, all the same."

He laughed at her proud refusal of his offer.

"What's the good of money unless one is helpful?" he asked.

She looked at him curiously as though he were something very unusual as a specimen of humanity.

"You must be very rich," she said. "Are you a millionaire or a saint?"

"Neither," he answered with another laugh. "But I have a bit of spare cash now and then. Just now I can spare enough to pay your fare to Tours, and save you from what may be a very unpleasant experience. Alone in Paris with the Germans arriving. Not amusing, *mademoiselle!*"

She agreed that it would not be amusing, but she refused to accept his offer unless he would take from her a little silver watch which she wore on her wrist.

"It goes now and again," she told him. "At the moment it is not going, but it will go if you sleep with it under your pillow—when you have a pillow."

It was a cheap little watch, but Hambledon accepted the change.

"I'll keep it as a souvenir," he said. "Here's the fare to Tours."

"No!" she cried with a vexed laugh. "It is five times the fare."

"You will need a little extra for food and so on. Besides, this is a very valuable little watch. It's worth an awful lot."

"A hundred and fifty francs when it was new," she assured him with strict honesty. She accepted that amount and then thanked him.

"Doubtless you are a millionaire and a saint," she said. "The combination is excellent. In any case, a thousand thanks."

She waved an *au revoir* to him when the column of refugees moved on again—the long-moving tide of carts and tired homeless people who had abandoned everything except a few belongings rather than live under German rule.

Some of the children who walked by their mothers were whimpering because of their weary little feet, though others trudged along sturdily. Edward relieved one of the mothers of a small boy whom she had been carrying pick-a-back, and hoisted him on his shoulder and strode along with him to the next stage. After that he carried a little girl who fell asleep on his shoulder.

"You are very kind," said Madeleine Delaroche, walking beside him for a while. "Armand and I are grateful to you for this kindness to our poor refugees. They talk among themselves about you. They say that American is a good friend of France. We shall not forget him."

"I'm a friend of France, all right," answered Edward with a sideways smile at this girl whose courage he admired. She was taking this long tramp bravely and spoke cheerfully to the peasants about her, making little jokes to keep up their spirit.

"I've lost sight of my fellow-American," said Edward presently. "What's happened to him?"

"He's leading an old farmhorse which doesn't want to go a step farther."

At night they bivouacked in fields along the roadside. Here and there a lantern gleamed through the translucent darkness of this night in early summer. It was warm and the air was scented with wild flowers and haystacks. The villages through which they had passed were all deserted except for a few old women who peered through their doorways and lean cats which prowled about the feet of the passers-by.

On the third night they were only ten kilometres from Paris. This fact dominated the thoughts of Chas Hunt, who was burning to get back.

"Paris tomorrow!" he exclaimed. "Jeepers Creepers! It seems a year since we left it."

"What then?" asked Madeleine, who understood his English, or some of it, though she spoke in French.

The party which had set out from the Château de Rollencourt had reassembled on a patch of grass by the roadside. Captain Hardy seemed in less pain after his rest on the farmcart, from which he had been helped down by Edward for a picnic meal with the others provided by the refugees. Jean Meudon had joined them with his daughter. Armand sat on the grass with his knees up and Madeleine leaned against him, using his knees for a back.

Hardy answered her with a laugh.

"A difficult question for some of us! I shall have to get some expert to look at my leg before I go much farther."

"I must get as far as a farm near Tours," said Armand. "My family is certainly there. My cousin Madeleine will come with me."

He hesitated for a moment and gave an invitation.

"My family would be glad to shelter you, *mon capitaine*, until there is a chance of escape."

Hardy looked at him doubtfully.

"I couldn't put them to such a risk," he said; "but it is a noble offer."

"It is meant seriously," said Armand.

"And it is an excellent idea," added Madeleine, with a friendly smile at this English officer, who was not particularly attractive at that time with his unshaven face and rough clothes.

Later that evening, after their meal, Armand and Madeleine wandered away to talk to some of the refugees. Chas Hunt went to sit with a family group with whom he had made friends, and by some magic of his own made them laugh now and then. Odette was nursing a sleeping child and perhaps found some unconscious consolation for the loss of her own babe. Her father had gone off to talk with a friend he had found among the others. Hambledon was alone with Christopher

Hardy on the patch of grass where they had had their meal. He heard Hardy give a slight groan after he had lain for some time with his eyes shut.

"Leg hurting?" asked Edward.

Hardy sat up and laughed uneasily.

"Unpleasant thoughts," he answered.

"Secret ones?"

Hardy shook his head and smiled.

"Nothing like that. No bite of conscience or pang of love. I've been thinking of what's going to happen to England. What's going to happen to my father and mother who live in South Kensington. What's going to happen in the sunny fields of Kent if Hitler sends his hordes that way. I wish to God I knew what was happening, and what's going to happen."

"Can't England take care of herself?" asked Edward. "Haven't you command of the sea? Isn't that good enough for your historic little island?"

Captain Hardy looked at him gravely though with a gleam of humour.

"My historic little island," he answered, "has lost that security which gave us a great advantage since William the Conqueror and 1066. The aeroplane has changed all that. From the French coast, where the Germans are now crouched ready for the next spring, I reckon it's about seven and a half minutes by air to the cliffs of Dover, and the Germans have swarms of planes against which we can put up only a small air force of brave boys with wings on their breasts, all of whom, no doubt, will die like little gentlemen."

He seemed to be speaking to himself when he uttered his next words.

"I wonder if those fellows got away. I don't see how they could get away."

"What fellows?" asked Hambledon.

Hardy raised his hand slightly and answered gloomily.

"The B.E.F. . . . Nine divisions of our best, hoofing it to Dunkirk while we were trying to hold the Germans away from the last line of escape. They are all we have in trained men. We have no other guns than theirs, no other tanks—and a pretty poor lot they were!—no other rifles and no other ammunition. If they haven't got away from Dunkirk —and where are the ships coming from?—there will be only untrained men standing on the coast-line of England and Scotland with sticks and stones to keep back the greatest military power in the world."

Hambledon raised his eyebrows.

"I didn't know it was as bad as that. Why did you go to war when you were so weak? I thought the British Empire was the mightiest combination on earth."

Hardy laughed again, but mirthlessly.

"Our statesmen put up a colossal bluff," he said. "Behind our façade of Empire we are weak and rotten. We guaranteed Poland and Roumania without strength enough to guarantee the beach at Brighton or the pier at Bournemouth. We had no army. We had let down the navy. Our Labour laddies in the House of Commons had for years preached pacifism until they shouted that we must stand up to the dictators. Old man Chamberlain—the man with the umbrella—made an eleventh hour attempt to prevent this war, and then weakened to the pressure from Left and Right, and declared war with nothing to fight it with, except nine divisions against the German two hundred and fifty for a start. Then our dear old generals, with last war's mentality and the unshaken belief that nine British divisions could get the German army on the run, put their whole bag of tricks—including all our pretty little guns and all our inefficient tanks, and all our brave boys—into a man-trap whose jaws were very strong and sharp. By what madness we were sent into Belgium God alone knows. Did we think the *brave Belges* could hold back the whole German army? Did we think a few French divisions up there could stand against the massed metal of those German robots? The inevitable happened, as I knew it would, not being a mental defective. Now we're in the soup. For the first time since the Norman Conquest our historic little island, as you call it so truly, is in danger of defeat, destruction and enslavement. Nothing can stop that except a miracle of God, and at the moment God seems to be pro-German."

Hambledon uttered the word "Gee!" and then spoke again. "I'm hoping for a miracle. I don't know England, but I do know what it has given to the world in law and liberty and inexhaustible genius. I wouldn't like to see it go under. No, sir!"

Hardy grinned at him.

"Thanks for those kind words," he said. "It's nice of an American to say them."

"Many Americans think the same," said Hambledon.

Hardy was silent and Hambledon watched his face—a clean-cut, young-looking face, in spite of its growth of beard. He sat with his hands drooping between his knees. Suddenly he raised his head and looked at Edward with an intense inner light in his blue eyes.

"Somehow I must get back to England," he said. "Whatever the risk, I must get back. I want to be with my own people. I want to die with them, if we have to die—in South Kensington or the Brompton road."

Armand and Madeleine came back. Chas Hunt slouched over from his family party by the wheels of a farmcart.

"Time we turned in," he said, yawning. "I'm dog-tired. I'll say I am."

Madeleine Delaroche was staring up at the sky and listening to a droning noise up there.

"They are coming again!" she said in a low voice. "Those black demons."

Darkness was creeping into the sky after a long and beautiful twilight and a golden sunset which had flung long shadows across the fields from the tall poplars bordering them. Stars were twinkling and a sickle moon was up. Seven black birds were visible up there. They made a wide circle and then dropped like hawks above a village less than half a kilometre away through which the refugees had passed. The camp, which had been settling down to sleep, suddenly stirred like an ant heap upturned by a spade. A woman shrieked as the first bomb fell on a little deserted village. There were cries of terror, and some of the refugees started running and threw themselves upon the earth. Only a few bombs were dropped before the black bats passed and there was quietude again.

"What was the use of it?" asked Hunt. "What do they think they gain by smashing a small hamlet whose people have fled?"

"It is a policy of terror," answered Armand. "It has no military purpose. It is to destroy civilian morale."

From the groups of refugees came shouts and curses. Children were crying. Elderly men held the heads of horses who had been frightened and were restless in their shafts.

"Assassins! . . . Bandits! . . . Killers of women and little ones!"

Presently they slept under the stars.

XII

THE MAIN COLUMN of refugees did not enter Paris but took to the roads going south. Before parting with them there were handclasps and cries of "*Bonne chance*, comrades!"

"Poor devils!" said Chas Hunt. "What's going to happen to them? I guess that's an unanswerable question. God alone knows."

A small group trudged into Paris. Among them were the two Americans, Armand and Madeleine, Jean Meudon with his daughter Odette, and Captain Christopher Hardy, escaped prisoner of war, who dragged one leg but found it less painful after this rest on the farmcart.

Jean Meudon and Odette said farewell at the end of the rue Lafayette. Meudon grasped Hambledon's hand first and spoke a few words of thanks.

"You dug the little one's grave," he said. "We shall never forget that kindness, *m'sieur*."

Odette wept a little on parting. It seemed to bring back her agony of grief for the dead child. She kissed Madeleine and then turned away sobbing.

Chas Hunt was the next to break away. This was near the Place de l'Opéra where they had sat down outside the Café de la Paix. The men were unshaven and unwashed, and plastered with dust. Edward glanced at his companions, who looked like typical refugees, and he felt the stubble on his own chin. Often he had sat here with parties of Americans, drinking cocktails and watching the passing traffic of Parisian life. Here he had sat with Olga during his time of passion for her. She had smoked Russian cigarettes over her cup of coffee and had teased him because of his American accent. Now, here he was, feeling as dirty as he looked, in a Paris awaiting the entry of its enemy. It was more deserted since he had left it. Few people passed, and none stopped to sit outside the Café de la Paix. Chas Hunt hailed a taxi-cab which was passing slowly and kept it waiting by the kerbstone while he said good-bye.

"I guess we'll meet again," he said in a casual way. "I must go and collect the latest news. Thanks a lot, Rollencourt. See you soon, Edward."

He raised a hand in salute, climbed into the cab, and was driven away to his newspaper office, not knowing whether it still functioned in a city which seemed dead.

The Café de la Paix still served coffee, for which Edward paid.

He spoke to the waiter who flicked his napkin over the table.

"What's the news?"

The waiter, who was an elderly, sad-eyed man, shrugged his shoulders slightly.

"Nothing good! The Germans are across the Seine. Everybody has left Paris. Everybody who can. Even the prostitutes and the good-for-nothings."

"What about the English?" asked Hardy. "Are they still at Dunkirk?"

The waiter stared at him for a moment and then answered gruffly:

"They got away. The English are very good at getting away and leaving other people in the lurch."

Hardy ignored this insult.

"By the Lord," he said, speaking to Edward, "if they got away it was a miracle."

It was only later that he heard of the miracle of the little ships—the old packet-boats and pleasure-yachts, and river steamers and every kind of craft, which had gone over to Dunkirk sands to take off those masses of men waiting patiently for their turn while German bombers flew overhead dropping high explosives in the sand dunes.

"It will be England's turn next," said the waiter grimly. "After the Germans have finished with us! . . ."

There were four people left at the little table outside the Café de la Paix. They were Edward, Armand de Rollencourt, Madeleine Delaroche and Kit Hardy, as Edward called him later.

"What are your plans?" asked Edward presently. "What can I do for you, if anything?"

"It is possible that there is still a train running to Tours," answered Armand. "After a little rest, Madeleine and I will try to get there somehow."

"And you?" asked Edward, looking at Hardy.

Hardy answered cheerfully but doubtfully:

"My problem is a bit difficult. I shall have to lie doggo. If the Germans march into Paris tonight it won't be too easy to get away. The fact is, my leg is very troublesome."

"I have a perfectly good car," said Edward. "It might help things if I drove you all down to Tours."

"That sounds like a miracle!" exclaimed Madeleine.

"It would save a great deal of fatigue," said Armand, in his formal way.

"That's fine," said Edward. "We'll do the trip together."

Suddenly he rose from his chair and said: "Excuse me a moment."

A friend of his was passing the Café de la Paix. It was William Ryan Smart of the American Embassy.

"Hullo, Bill!" shouted Hambledon.

Smart turned sharply and stared at him.

"Gosh!" he exclaimed. "You look like a refugee, and a lousy one at that."

"It's exactly what I am," said Edward. "But I'm going to have a bath and a shave. When are the Germans expected?"

"Within a few hours," answered Smart. "I've been left behind to clear up the mess."

After other remarks he remembered something.

"By the way, I was able to help your Jew friend, Paul Simon. He has all the necessary papers."

"Thanks a lot!" Hambledon was grateful for the service.

"Olga is going with him," said Smart. "They were married in a hurry. She did it for the sake of that anaemic Jew who said he wouldn't go without her. I gave them the tip and fixed it up. One of my little miracles!"

"Holy snakes!" exclaimed Edward, very much startled.

For a moment he felt stricken because Olga had married Paul Simon. But his life had become like a dream anyhow, a kind of waking nightmare in which there was no touch with the realities.

"Rapid work!" he said, after that moment of shock.

"I'll say it was a good idea. A great brain behind it."

William Ryan Smart nodded.

"Not much time to spare, old boy! See you later, maybe. I shouldn't advise you to stay in Paris."

He raised his hand and strode away—a young man in a hurry.

Hambledon returned to his companions.

"Better come to my studio," he said. "We mustn't get separated. We can all shake down and get a wash there and perhaps something to eat if I open a few cans."

He picked up another taxi-cab and drove to the Boulevard St. Germain, 27 bis, with his three newly-found friends, who needed his help and were glad to have it.

XIII

It was impossible for Hambledon to leave Paris. Hardy was suffering intense pain because of his wound and that evening became delirious again.

"It's a bad business," said Edward. "I'll have to get a doctor—if that's possible."

Hardy was lying on Edward's bed and spoke rambling words after flinging one arm over the bedside.

"It's all right, mother. . . . I shall come back all right. . . . I have a hunch about it. . . . I'm going to live to a ripe old age with my children and children's children. . . . Now, for goodness' sake, don't cry."

"Impossible to move him in this state," said Edward.

Armand and Madeleine were distressed. After some hesitation Armand decided that it would be best for them to take a train to Tours if that were still possible.

"No, no!" cried Madeleine. "It would be a dishonour. The English captain is our comrade. He has fought in France. He is an escaped prisoner of war. How can we leave him?"

"I also am in danger of becoming a prisoner of war," answered Armand. But he turned doubtfully to Hambledon and asked his advice.

"What do you think, my friend? Should we be dishonourable in trying to get to Tours? We would await you there."

"That's common sense," answered Edward. "It may be days before the captain is well enough to move."

Madeleine yielded reluctantly, and that evening Armand and his cousin took their chance of getting places on a train to Tours.

Before going, Armand spoke some emotional words to Edward.

"I look forward to seeing you again, my dear friend, if you will allow me to call you that. My heart is full of gratitude for your noble kindness and your splendid comradeship."

Hambledon laughed at this high praise and coloured up a little.

"I have done nothing, *mon lieutenant*."

Armand gripped his arms with both hands.

"You have done everything! Madeleine and I watched you with the refugees—with the old people and the little children. You were wonderful in your help and sympathy. You carried that crippled boy for many kilometres. You encouraged the young mothers. You made them even laugh. And to me you rendered a service which I shall never forget. You helped to carry my father to his grave. When the Germans came it was your coolness and courage which dealt with them. Madeleine and I thank you in the name of France."

Hambledon was embarrassed by all this and refused to take it seriously.

"My dear fellow, you make me blush. I behaved like any decent American, I hope."

"We owe much to you," said Madeleine, simply. Simply, also, she gave him her cheek to kiss.

"We are friends," she told him. "In a short time it is possible to make a great friendship, is it not?"

She went over to Christopher Hardy and put her hand on his forehead.

"He has a high temperature," she said. "I am full of pity for him."

Hambledon was left alone with the sick man. He was talking to himself again.

"One can't dodge these things in time of war. . . . Old Man Death has no pity for the young uns. . . . It's damn funny really when you come to think of it. . . . Play cricket one day. . . . Blue hell the next. . . . It makes me laugh."

He laughed quietly to himself in a queer, happy way, as though it were a good joke.

He spoke in what Edward imagined to be the Oxford accent, sounding a little affected to his American ear, though there could be no affectation in this delirious speech. Much of what he babbled was incomprehensible, but parts of it seemed to be addressed to his men in the recent fighting.

"We've got to stick it, you fellows. . . . We've got to hold on while the way is still open to Dunkirk. . . . Our lives won't be wasted if we can keep that way open for the other crowd. . . . All that's left to defend our homes . . . and our own women . . . Sergeant! For God's sake tell the men to stick it out. Never mind the dead. . . . Give the Jerries hell."

After that outburst he spoke more quietly and laughed again.

"My idea of paradise is fishing in a trout stream. Throw your fly, Peter. Artful beggars, aren't they? See that fellow in the shadow of the tree? Oh, very wily, indeed."

He laughed again with great good humour.

"That guy is in a bad way," said Hambledon to himself. "I'll say he is!"

He spent a lot of time looking up doctors in the telephone directory and then trying to get an answer from them.

Now and then a frightened voice answered, probably the concierge or some servant.

"Who is that?"

"Is the doctor at home?"

"There is no one here. Doctor Martin has left Paris."

"Hell," said Edward in perfectly good American.

At last he found one. It was Dr. Longeau in the Avenue des Champs-Elysées. He spoke abruptly.

"Why do you want me? Is it serious?"

"Very serious," answered Hambledon. "A question of life or death."

"I'm just about to leave Paris," said the doctor. He hesitated for a moment, and then said: "I will come at once."

He was a young man, very grave and nervous because of the state of Paris and his own private anxieties.

When he saw Christopher Hardy and heard his delirious talk he guessed at once that he was a British officer.

"An escaped prisoner of war?" he asked.

Edward nodded. "I'm telling you that in confidence, Doctor."

The doctor looked at him sombrely.

"It is very dangerous to hide a prioner of war. You also are English?"

"American."

"I do not want to get into more trouble than I have already," said the doctor. "I wish to get away before the Germans come."

Hambledon looked him squarely in the eyes.

"You are a doctor. You know your duty."

Dr. Longeau was not too pleased at this reminder.

"You ask me to take a grave risk, *m'sieur*."

He decided to take the risk after glancing at his wrist-watch, and felt Hardy's pulse and put his hand into this officer's shirt to feel the beat of his heart.

"He has a wound in the leg," said Edward.

"I shall have to cut away his trouser. Lend me a knife or a pair of scissors."

After cutting away the cloth he uttered an exclamation of horror.

"This is in a dreadful state. Filthy and neglected."

Hardy had bandaged himself with strips torn from a khaki shirt, now clotted with blood and sticking to the wound.

"*Cré Nom de Dieu!*" said the doctor in a voice of dismay. "I must do something at least to clean up this mess. Some warm water and linen, if you please."

Hambledon tore up one of his own shirts and produced the warm water. Hardy groaned heavily when his rags were removed and several times called out the name of Christ.

"It's all right, old man," said Edward. "It's all right."

"Have you any disinfectant?" asked the doctor. "There is danger here of gangrene. The wound is in a bad state. He ought to be taken to a hospital without delay."

"That would give him away," answered Edward. "Can't you operate here and now?"

"Quite impossible! My clinic is closed. My instruments are packed up. I leave Paris in half an hour."

But he washed and bandaged the wound, after giving Hardy a morphia injection which relieved his agony.

"That is something. But I advise you to get him to a hospital at the earliest possible moment."

"How much do I owe you?" asked Edward, when the doctor had washed his hands at the kitchen sink.

The young man shrugged his shoulders.

"It is not a case for a fee. In time of war . . ."

"Thanks a lot," said Edward.

Hardy lay in a stupefied sleep for several hours. When he awakened he seemed more at ease and was no longer delirious.

He stared at Edward, who was standing by his bedside.

"I seem to know your face," he said, "but I can't place it. . . . Oh, yes. I remember. . . . The road to Paris . . . the refugees. . . . I say, I'm afraid I'm giving you a hell of a lot of trouble, old man."

It was next morning that the Germans entered Paris.

XIV

HAMBLEDON STOOD BY the side of Chas Hunt and two or three other American newspaper men outside the Hôtel Crillon in the Place de la Concorde. He had left Hardy alone in his studio, still under the effect of morphia and sleeping quietly. Hunt had given him a telephone call and said: "They're coming. . . . They're already in the outskirts. . . . Meet me outside the Crillon."

Their coming was heralded by an earth tremor made by armoured cars. Bodies of German motor-cyclists rode ahead. They were followed by the armoured cars, Staff cars, and then by German troops in lorries. With their steel helmets low on the neck they looked a grim legion, inhuman in their expressionless faces, on which there was no exaltation of victory, no sign of curiosity, no gleam of intelligence. They might have been soldiers made of metal.

Few French people were there to see them and to suffer the first agony of their presence in Paris, this humiliation of defeat, this surrender of a city which to all Frenchmen is the centre of civilization.

"They look like a bunch of robots," said Chas Hunt.

Another newspaper man spoke in a low voice.

"It turns my blood cold."

Several military cars, long and grey with little pennants fluttering in front and English "tin hats" on their bonnets, stopped outside the Crillon, and a number of high officers jumped out. An Army General with a thin tight-lipped face stood in the centre of a group of officers who saluted and clicked heels to him. He rasped out a few words and strode into the hotel, followed by a few others. Those who were left outside suddenly became human and more easy in their attitude, lighting up cigars and talking to each other. Some of them glanced sideways at the group of American newspaper men, and presently an officer in the black uniform of the S.S. came to them and spoke, after saluting. He spoke in French.

"You are journalists?"

"American newspaper men," answered Chas Hunt coldly.

The S.S. officer spoke in English and smiled.

"I guessed that. You will have great news for your papers, gentlemen. This is an historic day."

No one answered him.

"I will not ask to see your passports," said the officer. "There will be plenty of time for all that later."

"When the Gestapo arrives?"

It was Hunt who asked this question in an unfriendly voice.

The S.S. officer smiled again.

"They have arrived. Everything is organized, of course. That is our German way. Good day, gentlemen. *Heil* Hitler."

He turned on his heel and joined the others.

An endless column of tanks and field-guns and armoured cars passed through Paris and flowed, like a stream of metal, up the Avenue des Champs-Élysées. Paris was in the hands of the enemy.

Hunt spoke to Hambledon.

"Come round to the office, Edward. We'll get some news over the radio. I want to hear what's happening in England. They must be feeling like hell about it. . . . All my English friends."

In the newspaper office on the first floor of a building in the Avenue de l'Opéra there was a great clicking of typewriters.

Hunt spoke to one of his colleagues who sat in his shirt-sleeves with a cigar in his mouth, typing rapidly.

"What's the latest, Johnnie?"

His friend was a young man who might have stepped off the cover of the *Saturday Evening Post*. He shifted his cigar slightly and stopped typing.

"The Germans are smashing through the Champagne. The Reynaud Cabinet is expected to resign and Pétain will take over the Government. It's a preliminary to asking for peace terms. England is preparing to be invaded. That is to say, the bottom's falling out of everything. Meanwhile, the Germans have taken over the Paris radio. I will say those guys don't lose much time."

Hunt turned on the radio in his own room. He switched on to the Paris station, now in German control.

A voice spoke in French with a slight German accent and announced that Herr somebody—Edward did not catch the name—would play a selection from Chopin. He played one of Chopin's melodies.

It was exquisite music, but the two Americans did not find it beautiful.

"It gives me a shiver down the spine," said Hunt.

Edward gave a little laugh.

"Queer people!" he exclaimed. "They like to think they're civilized. They must have put that pianist in an armoured car specially for this stunt. They think out everything in advance. I'll say they do."

Edward rose suddenly.

"I can't stay, Chas. I must get back to my wounded Captain. How am I going to get him out of Paris?"

"If you don't do it damn quick, you won't," answered Hunt.

Edward nodded.

"I guess it's tonight or never, and he's a very sick man."

He went back to his studio, where Hardy still slept.

It was at dawn next morning that Edward set out in his car with Christopher Hardy and took the road to Tours. Hardy had had a restless night but was able to stagger up and get into the car.

"How are you feeling?" asked Edward, when he had helped him on to the back seat.

"Weak on the pins but otherwise all right," answered Hardy cheerfully. "That cup of coffee you made has pulled me together wonderfully. I'm sorry to be such a damn nuisance. Very rough on you, old man; but I'm vastly grateful."

"No need for that," answered Edward. "Have a cigarette."

He tossed Hardy a packet of Camels and said: "If we're challenged you'd better lie doggo and speak your excellent French if any German questions you. I'll say I picked you up on the road among the refugees."

They were challenged at the Porte Maillot.

A harsh voice shouted out "Halt."

A German guard was here and an officer came up to the car and spoke in French.

"*Votre Passeport. . . . Votre carte d'identité.*"

"American," said Edward.

He took out his pocket-book and handed the officer his passport.

The officer examined it carefully.

"I have no instructions about Americans," he said. "I will let you pass. Who is that man with you?"

"A poor devil of a refugee," answered Edward. "I picked him up on the road. He has a bad leg."

"One cannot deal with the refugees," said the German officer. "They are like vermin on the roads. The French authorities ought to have stopped them. There is no order in France. One cannot fight a war when all the roads are choked by civilians. May I offer you a cigar?"

He held out his case with a friendly gesture.

"No, thanks," said Edward, "but I only smoke cigarettes."

The officer laughed.

"Then you do not smoke."

He spoke a word or two in German to his men, who made room for the car to pass.

It was a minute or two before Hardy spoke from the back of the car.

"Marvellous," he said. "I broke into a cold sweat when we were challenged."

"I'll say I had an uneasy moment," answered Edward.

On the road to Tours Hardy was talkative from time to time. His mind was fixed upon England and its state of peril.

"With France out of the war," he said, "we're alone, and damned weak."

"You still have a strip of sea round you," said Edward. "Britannia rules the waves, doesn't she?"

"They may come by air," said Hardy. "Parachutists and airborne troops. God! I wish I could get to England before it happens."

He spoke of his family. His father was a solicitor. He had won the M.C. in the last war—on the Somme. He was a bit of a pacifist, having been through the last show when all his pals had been killed. He had been a fervent supporter of the League of Nations. All his dreams and ideals had gone down into the mud because of Hitler.

"My mother," said Hardy presently, "is the best woman in the world."

"All mothers are," answered Edward.

Hardy laughed.

"But mine is exceptional. Extraordinarily intelligent. Wonderfully well poised. Never fusses or frets. She has the spirituality of an angel."

"That's fine," answered Edward, with his eye on the road.

"Before I joined up in this war," said Hardy presently, "I was one of our little idealists. I suppose it was my father's influence partly. I was all for international co-operation and collective security. That failed, and was shown to be an illusion when we didn't take drastic action against Mussolini for his attack on Abyssinia. That led Hitler to think he could get away with anything, and Mussolini to come in on his side now that France is collapsing. We have made many ghastly mistakes ever since the last war. Now all hell is let loose, and we share part of the guilt."

"I have to include my own country," answered Edward. "We quitted the League of Nations and left the baby on the door-step. Wasn't that the beginning of failure?"

"I agree," said Hardy. "It's good of an American to say so."

Edward laughed.

"Some Americans are pretty critical of their own Government. I'm one of the critics. I think one cause of World War II was the high tariff wall we put up against European goods. That caused the economic blizzard and German inflation and general poverty. Out of that Hitler arrived. That's how I read it."

So they talked on the road to Tours, where presently they caught up again with a mass of refugees stretching for miles ahead.

"Now what are we going to do?" asked Edward. "If we hug this road we shall be a week or more on the way to Tours."

Ahead of them was the usual slow-moving tide of farmcarts, handcarts, wheelbarrows, bicycles, ancient motor-cars, and foot-sloggers. Babies wailed, wheels screeched. Hairy old horses plodded on, led by old men and women and young girls.

"Better take a chance and plunge into the side roads," said Edward. He escaped the refugees by turning into narrow country roads which twisted and turned into small French hamlets and sometimes led them into fields and farmyards. The car lunched and bumped on these rough tracks and several times Hardy groaned heavily because of his wound, but laughed courageously when Edward said: "Sorry, captain!"

"Don't you mind me," said Hardy. "Every mile you make increases my chance of escape and brings me nearer to England."

An hour later Edward said "Hell!" with great annoyance. Once again he had driven into a farmyard at the end of a winding lane. An elderly man in a blue béret and labourer's clothes was astonished to see a powerful car come into his yard. It was as though he thought the Germans had arrived.

"I am making for Tours," said Edward in French. "I am trying to avoid the main roads because of the refugees. I am an American. My friend here is English."

The farmer looked relieved and the suspicious fear left his eyes.

"Everybody is on the way to Tours," he said. "Hundreds of thousands of refugees. Come into my farmhouse, gentlemen. I still have a little wine and my wife will make some coffee for you."

It was a good invitation. Both Edward and Hardy were in need of refreshment. The farmer's wife greeted them in a friendly way, but had tears in her eyes when she spoke of the state of France.

"They will be here soon, those bandits," she said. "No part of France will escape from them. They will swarm over us like locusts."

Later, she wept a little when she told them that her eldest son had been killed near Sedan and that the other was missing behind the mystery of the war in Champagne, from which no news came except the tale of disaster.

"One day," said Edward, "France will rise again. These black days will pass."

"Never," said the farmer. "France is at the end of her history as a great nation. We cannot suffer two wars like this. All our young men are being killed. Our best blood is drained to the dregs."

There was a girl standing at the back of the kitchen. She cried out angrily.

"Father, how dare you say such things? They are untrue. They are abominable. This gentleman has told you the truth. France will rise again. Nothing can kill the soul of France."

"Perhaps you are right," said the farmer. "I speak in the hour of despair. Another glass of wine, *messieurs?*"

They drank another glass of wine, and when they left the farmer shook hands with them and his grip was hard.

"You are friends of France," he said. "That is enough."

Into the narrow roads they went again. Edward steered by the sun, taking a southerly course, twisting and turning, and often getting into mere cart-tracks so that he had to hark back again. Hardy became feverish again and was obviously suffering great pain. But whenever he spoke it was with forced cheerfulness and encouragement to his American friend.

"I'm all right. Carry on, old man. We shall soon be there."

Soon was an optimistic word. It was not until early the following day, having driven all night, that Edward drove through Tours, where an army of refugees was encamped in the streets. They came to an old place, half farmhouse and half château, ten kilometres or so beyond.

He had been directed to this place by Armand de Rollencourt, who came running down a flight of stone steps as the car drove up.

"You are here!" he cried. "It is wonderful. We had a terrible journey from Paris. Madeleine is now in bed."

A tall young girl stood at the top of the steps. Edward watched her as she came down. To his painter's eye she looked like the portrait of herself by Vigée Lebrun.

She held out her hand to Edward when he got out of his seat and stood by the car.

"This is my sister, Lucile," said Armand.

"My brother has spoken very much about you," she said. "My mother and I wish to thank you."

"I have done nothing," said Edward. "This is my friend, Captain Hardy."

Hardy had managed to get out of the car with the help of Armand. He looked ill and exhausted, but he pulled off his old béret as he took Lucile's hand.

"I'm afraid I'm a dangerous guest," he told her in his very good French. "I must get away as soon as possible."

"Not too soon," said Lucile. "We are going to nurse you."

"Then I shall never want to go," answered Hardy.

Lucile laughed and shook her head.

"Oh, I'm not such a good nurse as all that."

They both laughed rather shyly.

"My mother is anxious to welcome you," said Armand.

He led the way into the house and then into a room comfortably furnished with chintz-covered chairs and one or two small tables, with a piano by an open window looking out to a farmyard and, beyond that, to the old roofs of a French village with a little church and market-place, and an old inn called Le Cheval Blanc. It was the village of Grancourt Nôtre-Dame.

In the room was a lady dressed in black. At first sight she looked too young to be the mother of Armand and Lucile, though there were little lines about her eyes and mouth and a few silver threads in her black hair.

"My mother," said Armand, with a note of tenderness and devotion in his voice.

Madame de Rollencourt held out her hand to Edward—a thin, transparent hand which was, he noticed, cold to his touch.

"I am very glad you have come," she said. "Armand has told me of your great kindness and friendship."

She guessed, and it was not difficult to guess, that he was the tall young American of whom her son had spoken, and then she turned to Christopher Hardy and greeted him charmingly.

"You are the English officer who escaped. You must rest here and get well. I hope your wound is less painful, *mon capitaine*."

"Oh, it is not too bad," answered Hardy. "But I must get away before I bring trouble here."

"You speak French beautifully," said Madame de Rollencourt, as though astonished that any English officer should speak French so well. She did not seem to be afraid of any trouble he might bring.

"The enemy is still a long way from Tours. There is a little time for us to think things out. We won't let them take you again. Somehow we must arrange that."

"No, indeed!" cried Lucile. "We won't let you be recaptured, *m'sieur*. You will be safe with us here even if we have to hide you away."

"Nothing is safe," said Armand, gloomily. "In a few days they may be here. . . . But we must get our English friend to bed. He looks very ill."

Christopher Hardy looked very faint. He swayed a little until he grabbed the back of a chintz-covered chair.

"Excuse me," he said. "I feel rather stupid."

Edward was quick to hold him and prevent a fall.

"Help me to carry him upstairs," said Armand. "We must get a doctor instantly."

"I will take my bicycle," said Lucile. "I will dash down to Dr. Moineau."

She went quickly out of the room, while Edward stooped to put his arms round Christopher Hardy, who was in a state of collapse.

Armand and Hambledon staggered up some broad stairs to a barely-furnished room, where they laid him down on a four-poster bed.

The journey was too much for him, maybe," said Edward. "I'm getting scared."

Madame de Rollencourt had come into the room noiselessly.

She put her hand on Hardy's forehead.

"Poor young man!" she said in a low voice. "He has a high fever. We must wait for Dr. Moineau."

They waited by Hardy's bedside for Lucile to bring back the doctor.

Hardy was talking to himself incoherently.

It was the first scene in this old farmhouse which afterwards Edward Hambledon came to know with an intimate knowledge, touched by wonderment that by the oddest chance of Fate he should be living here, dangerously, with two women sharing a secret drama with him. He came to know every crack and creak in the floor-boards. He came to know every house in the village, every cobblestone in the market-place, and the path which led to the wood where nightingales sang, and the chalk quarry beyond, where he went with Lucile, and the road to Tours, and the ten-acre field where at night, later in history, agents of de Gaulle landed from the sky, bringing secret cargoes. He had once belonged to Massachusetts, where his family worried about him. Now, during this fantastic and dream-like period of his life, he belonged, body and soul, to this remote hamlet in France, very quiet but not inactive during a World War.

XV

DR. MOINEAU, WHO was an old man now retired from a hospital in Tours, took a serious view of Hardy's leg. Gangrene had set in, he said. The wound had been terribly neglected. The leg would have to come off if the young man's life was to be saved. He would have to be taken to hospital without delay.

"But, my dear doctor," said Armand, who was very distressed at this verdict, "if we take him to the hospital we may hand him over to the enemy, who will undoubtedly enter Tours before long. We have not hidden from you that he is an English officer."

The little old doctor shrugged his shoulders.

"Better for him to be a prisoner of war than a dead man."

"That is very true," said Lucile, who was present at this conference in the sitting-room of the old farmhouse, with her mother and Edward. "But it would be better still if he remained alive and free."

"You ask too much, my dear," answered the old doctor.

Lucile did not agree with that.

"He might pass as a Frenchman. He speaks excellent French."

"He must have his papers," said Armand, doubtfully.

"A French *carte d'identité*. How is that possible?"

It was that question and the answer to it which was the beginning of an organization in which Hambledon found himself deeply involved in course of time. It began in this village of Grancourt Nôtre-Dame. It spread in an underground way to Tours and other towns. It had many agents, among whom were Lucile de Rollencourt, Madeleine Delaroche, Dr. Moineau, the village priest, and Edward himself.

The little old doctor pushed back the black silk cap which covered his bald head.

"That is not beyond possibility," he said, with the cunning look of an old peasant.

"Pierre Prunier, who was my gardener and handy-man, died last night from *angina pectoris*, which exempted him from military service. He will not need his *carte d'identité* and other papers. They will not be demanded by St. Peter at the gate of Heaven. St. Peter will say: 'Pass, Pierre Prunier, good gardener and honest man.' His *carte d'identité* and other papers will serve very well for this English officer while he is in hospital. If the Boches arrive they will suspect nothing."

There was a moment's silence in the room, and then Lucile gave a little laugh.

"Brilliant!" she exclaimed. "It's a magnificent idea, dear doctor. And it is most convenient that Pierre Prunier died last night."

"It's dangerous," said Armand thoughtfully. "But one must take the risk."

"My little idea seems to meet with approval," said the doctor with a chuckle. "So I am not such an old fool after all. Eh?"

It was with the papers of Pierre Prunier that Captain Christopher Hardy was taken that afternoon to the hospital in Tours, ten kilometres away. He was taken in a farmcart in which straw had been laid by Edward and Lucile. Dr. Moineau sat in it with the wounded man, who was now unconscious. It would be necessary, he said, to have a word with the house surgeon and the matron. They were friends of his and he could trust them. It was necessary to trust them and perhaps others like the village *curé*, who had known Pierre Prunier. They were good patriots. They would not betray him.

Hambledon stood on the wheel of the cart to take a last look at Christopher Hardy before his leg was amputated. He felt a sense of comradeship with this young fellow, whom he had known such a short time. In spite of the wound in his leg, which must have caused him horrible pain, he had been gay and gallant. He had charming manners and was a good type.

That was Lucile's opinion also.

"He is charming, your English officer," she said. "It will be terrible for him to lose a leg."

"Very bad luck," said Edward.

Lucile walked back with him silently to the house until at the gate of the farmyard she turned to him and spoke a few words.

"There is much in that idea of Dr. Moineau," she said thoughtfully. "Dead men's papers. We might extend that plan to others who are trying to escape."

"Are there enough dead men to go round?" asked Edward with a laugh.

He regretted that jest when she answered in tragic words.

"Thousands of our soldiers have been killed. There is no lack of dead in France. You helped to bury my own father."

"Forgive me," said Edward. "I was clumsy."

"No, no!" she exclaimed. "I do not reproach you. I know that you are a friend of France."

"Always," he assured her. "Here's my hand on it, lady."

He was glad to have her hand in his for a moment—a beautiful hand which one day he would like to paint or draw. He liked the look of her standing there in the gateway of the old farmhouse. That was a good background—the old house with its mansard roof and stone walls and mullioned windows. She might have been a lady of France when Du Bellay was writing his sonnets.

Her eyelashes quivered a little and she smiled at him.

"Why do you look at me so intently?" she asked. "Have I straws in my hair after packing up the cart?"

"I'm a painter," he told her. "I would like to do a sketch of you one day, just here at this gate."

A faint colour crept below her skin, and she laughed.

"I have never had my portrait painted. I should dislike to spoil a good canvas."

"You wouldn't," he assured her, "but I might."

A few evenings later a small group of people were in the sitting-room of this old farmhouse in the village of Grancourt Nôtre-Dame listening to the radio, which Armand had switched on to the German-controlled Paris station.

"It is, of course, all lies," he said.

Madeleine Delaroche had come over from Tours on her bicycle and was much distressed to hear that Captain Hardy had had his leg amputated and was in a grave state.

"It is too terrible!" she cried. "He is all that one thinks of the best type of the English officer and gentleman, *sans peur et sans reproche*."

Dr. Moineau had brought the news about Hardy.

"The operation has been successful," he said; "but his condition is not too good. They are anxious about him."

Another visitor had come to spend the evening with Madame de Rollencourt. It was the village *curé*, Gaston Berger, who had fought in the last war as a sergeant of artillery and was now a man past sixty with a lean face and humorous mouth and dark eyes which were lit by an inner flame. He was one of those who knew that Hardy had been registered at the hospital under the name of Pierre Prunier.

"We are conspirators!" he said with a laugh, after taking the hand of Madame de Rollencourt and holding it against his heart for a moment as though he loved her and was full of pity for her.

"If the Germans find out, we shall all be put into a concentration camp—at least, the doctor and myself. But I am prepared to take the risk."

"We are all ready to take the risk," said Lucile. "Many risks to help those who have fought against our enemy."

The priest looked at her with a smile.

"You have courage, *mademoiselle!* It was not the women of France —or our young girls—who failed in courage or loyalty. It was the old men who failed—our political leaders in that cesspool of Paris."

"Listen," said Armand urgently.

They listened intently to some words spoken over the radio. Edward Hambledon listened, but his eyes roved to the faces about him. It was as though those words over the microphone had stricken them with horror, like a sentence of death upon those they loved.

They heard an old man's voice, very sad and tremulous. It was the voice of Marshal Pétain.

"People of France, it is with a heavy heart that I say we must cease to fight. . . . I have asked for terms of peace. . . . France will not accept shameful terms. . . . France will preserve her dignity, courage, and faith in the future."

Armand was the first to break a tragic silence.

"We have surrendered. . . . Oh, my God!"

"It is terrible," said Madame de Rollencourt in a low voice. Edward noticed that her long thin hands plucked at her black dress. She sat very still even when she wept, unconscious of the tears which trickled down her pale face.

Lucile sprang up and cried out in a loud voice:

"It is shameful! Our armies are betrayed. That old man has betrayed us all. We could have fought on. I will fight on. I have not surrendered."

Edward looked at this girl. She flung back her head as though in defiance of the whole German *Wehrmacht*. Then suddenly she broke down and flung herself on to a chintz-covered sofa and wept with passion.

"That girl has the spirit of Jeanne d'Arc," thought Edward. "All the tradition of France is in her blood. I'm darned sorry for her. This surrender of France is terrible for a girl like that, with her pride and courage. It is terrible for all of them. I ought not to be here. It's like watching the martyrdom of a people, as a mere onlooker."

These thoughts passed through his mind in a tick of time.

"Calm yourself, Lucile," said Madame de Rollencourt, rising from her own chair and sitting on the edge of the sofa with her own wet cheek against Lucile's. "Let us at least follow Marshal Pétain's call to dignity and courage and faith in the future. You say you have not surrendered. Be brave then, my dearest."

Madeleine Delaroche had crossed the room to Lucile and bent down to put an arm about her. But then she stood up straight and Edward, watching her, saw that there were little flames in her eyes.

"I am with Lucile," she said. "I, too, refuse to surrender. I mean in mind and soul. I will do everything against the Germans. We women must put up a moral resistance against them and do everything in our power to weaken them and humiliate them. We must work secretly for the day of liberation."

It was the old doctor who asked a question with a kind of despair:

"How will it come, that day of liberation? I see only enslavement ahead. Who will fight for us? England? England will never fight for us, and is she not our hereditary enemy? In any case, is not England doomed also? Where is their army? Where is their strength? When Hitler invades them they will be defenceless. It is perhaps the end of European civilization. Hitler and his devils have all of us at their mercy. It makes me a little sceptical of God. Where, then, is God? Why has He abandoned us? Why has He allowed Evil to prevail? Tell me that, *mon père*. Difficult to answer, eh?"

The priest had been sitting with bowed head at the news of Pétain's surrender, or rather his request for terms of peace. He had only glanced silently at Lucile with sympathy in his eyes when she flung herself down and wept. He had listened to Madeleine with a tragic smile But now he turned to the doctor and spoke half-humorously and half-angrily, and his dark eyes glowed with their inner light.

"You are a foolish old sceptic, doctor, as I have always known you to be. You blame these things upon the good God. Do you not understand that men have to pay the price of sin and folly? France has to pay the price of much sin and innumerable follies. We have wallowed in corruption since the last war—our politicians, our industrialists, our parties on the Left and on the Right, greedy for their own power, forgetful of France. We have opened the gates to the enemy. Should we be surprised or blame *le bon Dieu* when the enemy walks in? You are a good doctor, my dear old friend. You and I have played many games of chess together. I know your humanity, and your love of those who suffer and need your help, which you give without payment. But as a theologian you are unqualified and as a philosopher you are very limited in knowledge. France will have to suffer this agony in order to be purged of a thousand poisons which have crept into her political and social life. France will have to be crucified in order to regain her soul and reveal her renaissance. You say we have no one to fight for us. One day we will fight for ourselves. I am impressed by our young ladies here. They are so young and we are so old. But did they not both say something which is a promise—that France will rise again. 'I refuse to surrender,' said Mademoiselle Lucile—our beautiful Lucile, 'I have not surrendered,' said Mademoiselle Madeleine. She spoke of moral resistance. She is right. That must be our attitude and resolve. It is what I shall tell my faithful little flock—not too faithful some of them, like you, my old friend—and it is to those words that I shall dedicate myself. Moral resistance to German tyranny. Moral resistance to their evil philosophy. Moral resistance to their secret police and the cruelties they will impose upon us. I go even further with these two young ladies. If I can hinder the enemy in any Christian way by helping their victims to escape, by a secret work of rescue, by encouraging ultimate resistance and liberation even by force of arms.—Was I not a soldier of the last war?—I will do so at any cost and any risk, even if the end of it is death. There are many others in this village of Grancourt who will work with me. I know them. I can trust them—old Jean Marchant the postman, Paul Longeau in the Reine Jeanne, Bertrand Gaspard, my sexton, and other men here who fought with me at Verdun. And you, my dear doctor, I number you among them. Have you not already helped one poor fellow to escape—that young Englishman who now lies in hospital with the *carte d'identité* of Pierre Prunier?"

Dr. Moineau had listened to this eloquence without interruption but with little gestures and grimaces, and once or twice a short harsh laugh.

"This is a sermon," he answered. "That is why I avoid High Mass on Sunday. I don't like being preached at by a fellow who went to school with me and whose shins I used to kick. . . . All the same, Gaston, I agree with you. You can count on me for any dirty work against the Boches."

"We have surrendered," said Armand, in a low tremulous voice. "Oh, my God! . . . Oh, my God!"

He rose from his chair and walked stiffly out of the room.

Edward also rose and went up to his room and sat on the side of a bedstead, thinking things out.

"I wonder if I ought to quit France," he thought. "Wouldn't it be more sensible to get away while the going's good, and enjoy the peace of Massachusetts where my family must be wondering what in hell I'm doing?"

He thought that out for a long time. But these thoughts urged him to postpone that journey. "I feel at home in France," he thought. "I like the French people. I'd be glad to stay with them a bit in their time of trouble. I might help a few of them to escape the clutches of the enemy. And I'm darned interested in all this. It's history in the making. It's an almighty drama of which I've only seen the prelude. I don't see why I should hurry back to peace and plenty with no definite purpose in life except a game of golf and a swim in Assawampsett Lake, and chit-chat at cocktail parties in Boston and New York. Besides, Mademoiselle Lucile de Rollencourt has something about her which is very unusual, and I want to do a study of her head."

He lit a Camel cigarette—one of his last—as he sat on the edge of the bedstead in an old French farmhouse, three thousand miles away from his home in Massachusetts.

XVI

During these days and nights they hung on to the wireless news, sometimes from Radio Paris but often from the B.B.C. in London, which Edward interpreted. A hundred times Armand, who knew no English, asked the question: "What are they saying? . . . What does it mean?"

Strange things were spoken by the voices of these English announcers. Winston Churchill, the Prime Minister, had offered a solemn union with France. The two countries would pool their resources. There would be a common citizenship, if France would keep up the struggle against the enemy of both peoples.

"Astonishing idea," said Armand. "I do not understand it."

"It's too late, anyhow," answered Edward.

It was too late. Marshal Pétain, who was head of the French Government after the resignation of Reynaud and his Cabinet, was negotiating terms of Peace with Hitler. They were almost completed, according to the Paris radio, though here and there fighting still went on.

Another voice reached this old farmhouse in France from England. It was a voice speaking in French, vibrant, strong, resolute. It was a call to all Frenchmen from a man named de Gaulle.

"*I tell you that France is not lost. France is not alone—not alone—not alone. She has a vast Empire behind her. She can unite with the British Empire which holds the seas. She can utilize to the full, as England is doing, the vast industrial resources of the United States. . . . Whatever happens, the flame of French resistance must not, and shall not, be extinguished. . . . France will never surrender her fleet. I, General de Gaulle, now in London, invite all Frenchmen who arrive in England, or who can escape to this country, to get in touch with me.*"

He made a stirring and moving appeal for active and enduring resistance until the liberty of France was restored.

Armand de Rollencourt listened to those words with profound emotion.

"That is the leadership we want," he said. "Thank God there is still a Frenchman who upholds our pride and spirit. We must rally round him. We will make an army of resistance under his command. I must go to England. I must join him. He gives us new hope."

"Who is he?" asked Edward. "I don't know much about him."

Armand was astonished at this ignorance.

"If they had listened to General de Gaulle we should not have lost this war. For years he has been the advocate of mechanized warfare. Tanks, more tanks, and still more tanks. Infantry moving rapidly in motor vehicles. Guns on tractors. A mobile army heavily armoured against guns and shell fire. He wrote a book on this subject—a masterpiece. The Germans adopted his ideas. They have won the war because of them. But de Gaulle was ignored by our High Command. He was given a subordinate position. His genius was thrown away by those *gaga* old men whose minds have not moved since the last war. I must go to England. I must enlist in his army of resistance."

He strode across the room as though already on his way to England.

There was a dreadful hour when the news came of the capitulation and that theatrical scene which Hitler had staged in the very railway coach at Compiègne which Foch had used in 1918 when Germany surrendered. He had made certain concessions. The occupation of France was to be only partial. There was to be an unoccupied region under French control. It was in return for a pledge given by Pétain, a pledge of French collaboration with Germany in the economic sphere.

That word *collaboration* was like poison to Armand and his family.

"Shameful!" he cried in a harsh voice. "It is an acceptance of economic slavery. Collaboration with the Boches? Never."

"It is dishonour," said Lucile. "We should be dishonoured for ever."

Madame de Rollencourt had another thought which was not comforting.

"According to the terms," she said, "we are just inside the occupied region. We shall have the Germans here."

Armand looked at her and for a moment his face was ashen grey.

"That is a ghastly thought," he said. "Yes, you are right, *maman*. The line will be drawn south of us. We have no luck."

Edward saw Lucile grow pale, but she laughed nervously.

"When they come," she said, "it will not be amusing. I can think of nothing more horrible."

"We must behave with dignity," said her mother. "Nothing they can do to us must make us lose that. Let us show them that we have an old tradition of pride and self-respect."

Lucile laughed again.

"I shall never have your wonderful dignity, *maman*. I belong to another generation. Our manners are not so good."

She raised her hands—those hands which Edward thought beautiful—and the laughter faded out of her eyes.

"Why do I talk nonsense at this time? In my heart I am weeping. France has surrendered. We are in the hands of the enemy. It will be a long agony for all of us."

She turned to Edward, who had been silent during this time of tragic news.

"This is not amusing for you, *m'sieur*," she said. "Let us go for a little walk and forget our miseries because the sun still shines and the sky is blue over France."

"I should like to," answered Edward. "It's a good day for a walk."

It was a pleasant walk he had with Lucile de Rollencourt. They went through the village of Grancourt Notre-Dame with its old houses, red-roofed, and a little market-place. Everyone knew her and gave her a greeting. Old men doffed their bérets and said, "*Bonjour, mademoiselle.*" A few women in the market-place smiled at her, and she raised her hand and smiled back, and now and then stopped to talk with one of them. The *curé* met them and raised his black felt hat.

"Sad news, Lucile," he said. "But General de Gaulle has spoken brave and noble words."

He spoke a few words to Edward.

"We are glad to have an American in this village of Grancourt. We have not forgotten their aid in the last war. Your men will be here again before this one ends."

"That's a hope," said Edward. "But we shall be late again."

"We are going to walk away from tragic thoughts," said Lucile. "For an hour or so we are going to pretend that life is as beautiful as God wishes it to be in the loveliness He has made for us. Is that a good Christian thought, M'sieur le Curé?"

She spoke in a smiling way, though half an hour ago she had wept in her heart.

"I give that thought my blessing," said the *curé*. "I would like to come with you and show our friend the charm of our countryside, but I have to visit Madame Monnet, who is in a bad state because her son was killed at Sédan. A pleasant *promenade*, my children."

He raised his black felt hat and passed on.

"I will take you to the Bois des Fées on the little hill over there," said Lucile. "In the distance you will see the roofs and towers of Tours. The view from the little wood is enchanting."

"It has an enchanting name," said Edward. "I hope we see some fairies."

They did not see any fairies but Edward Hambledon had a sense of enchantment, on this June day, with a hill-top view of Tours with its towers and roofs faintly pencilled against the blue sky, far away, over a lovely landscape where the crops were growing high for that year's harvest. Down below were village spires half-hidden by the full foliage of June and long straight roads lined with tall poplars. Sweet sounds came up to them—a church bell ringing, the clink of an anvil, a cuckoo calling. Sunlight glinted through the wood, the Bois des Fées, and spangled the carpet of last year's leaves. Tall foxgloves grew in the ditches, and Lucile picked some honeysuckle from a thicket.

"It all seems steeped in peace," she said. "There are no horrors visible. Beauty still lives in France."

"Let's forget all the tragedy," said Edward. "I'd like to sit down on this bank and talk of beauty and pleasant things."

"That will be difficult," answered Lucile. "Unpleasant things keep crowding into one's mind. But I shall be glad to sit down and watch the sunlight and the shadows passing across those fields."

They sat down on the bank and Lucile gathered some flowers from the grass by her side and put them to her lips.

"They are very sweet," she said. "They are the little jewels of God. Our Lord loved the lilies of the field."

"Tell me their names," answered Edward.

She told him the old French names and he tried to remember them. *La collerette de la Vierge . . . Le chèvre-feuille . . . La Marguerite . . . L'eglantine . . .*

"They come into our old songs and poetry," she told him. "I remember some nursery rhymes about them."

"Let me hear them," said Edward.

She had a good memory for those nursery rhymes and he liked to hear them because there was music in her voice and her diction was exquisite, he thought.

"One day I must learn to speak French without an American accent," he said. "It must sound horrible to you."

"Not in the least horrible," she told him, "but just a little amusing. It's mostly the intonation. You know all the words and are very fluent. If you like I will cure that accent. You have a good ear, *m'sieur*."

"I'd like to be taught, *mademoiselle*," he told her.

"Say this little *chanson* after me," she suggested.

"*Fais dodo Colas mon p'tit frère,*
Fais dodo t'auras du lolo.
Maman est en haut qui fait du gâteau,
Papa est en bas qui fait du chocolat.
Fais dodo Colas mon p'tit frère
Fais dodo t'auras du lolo."

He had his first lesson and did not resent her laughter when his American intonation kept coming through.

"Tell me about your family," she said presently. "I want to know more about you. At present you have a background of mystery."

He told her about his home in Massachusetts, and gave her character studies of his father and mother, and that tall brother whom they called Tiny, and Penny his sister, who was mad on horses, and the great lake of Assawampsett where, in the days before the landing of the Pilgrim Fathers, Red Indians had the great loneliness to themselves so that even now one felt their unseen presence in the silent woods.

"Why do you stay in France?" she asked. "Why don't you go back to this beautiful home where there is peace beyond the reach of Hitler?"

"I'm in no hurry to go," he answered. "France has caught hold of me somehow, and I can't tear myself away just yet. I'm an observer of world history. Besides, I want to paint you one day. I can't go before I've done that."

She turned to smile at him and for the second time when he had spoken of painting her a little colour crept into her cheeks.

"Then you must hurry," she said. "You must paint me before the Germans come." She glanced at a little wrist-watch and gave a cry.

"Can it be possible? Six o'clock! We must go back, or *maman* will be anxious."

"It has been a golden hour," said Edward. "We must have more like it as an escape from tragic stuff."

"It has been very agreeable," said Lucile, demurely. "For a little while I have forgotten the surrender of France."

They walked back through the wood of the fairies.

XVII

CAPTAIN CHRISTOPHER HARDY, whom Edward learned to call Kit, was brought back in an ambulance from the hospital in Tours where Edward had visited him several times. There had been no trouble about that, and it was an open secret with the matron and nurses that "Pierre Prunier" was an escaped English officer who had been wounded near Dieppe in the fighting up north.

He had had another visitor. It was Madeleine Delaroche, who had brought him fruit, flowers, and books. He was still very weak when he came back to Grancourt Notre-Dame and lay upstairs in a small bedroom looking out to the farmyard and the fields, but he made a joke now and then about the loss of his leg and had not lost his sense of humour when it was lopped off.

One thing worried him. He revealed it to Edward, who sat by his bedside one afternoon after fixing up a small wireless which he had bought for him in Tours at an extravagant price.

"My night nurse was an angel," he said, "but very anti-British. She knew perfectly well that I was English, but she didn't disguise her belief that the retreat to Dunkirk was a betrayal of France, and that we had dragged France into the war and then let her down. She wasn't the only one. Most of the patients in my ward talked like that. I had to keep quiet as I was posing as Pierre Prunier, but I didn't like it, my dear Hambledon. The blood of my undistinguished ancestors was at boiling-point sometimes."

Edward nodded.

"I've heard a lot of that, mostly in the cafés of Tours after paying you my visits. They're all cursing the English as the main cause of their defeat. I guess it's natural to want a whipping-boy to cover their own humiliation. There was quite a scene in the Café des Valois when the news came that the British Fleet had sunk French battleships at Mers el Kebir."

"Well," exclaimed Hardy, "it doesn't sound too good—turning our guns on our own Allies."

"They made pretty good offers to Admiral Darlan," said Edward. "He could join the British Navy or go to a neutral port. Our friend Armand says the English were perfectly justified. They mean to carry on the war alone, and the surrender of the French fleet to the enemy wouldn't help things. De Gaulle takes the same view, according to his broadcast speeches."

Hardy groaned again.

"Now that I have lost my leg I'm on the scrap-heap as a fighting man. I'm utterly useless now in England or anywhere else. I feel very low in spirit, my dear Hambledon, in spite of my little efforts to make a joke now and then."

He cheered up again because of a speech he heard that evening on his wireless set, which he could tune in to the B.B.C. It was a speech by Winston Churchill to the British people.

"*We have the honour to be alone. . . . We will fight on the hills and in the valleys. . . .*"

"Great stuff!" said Hardy, raising himself in bed a little. "It's like listening to Bill Shakespeare, Nelson, and the younger Pitt. Thank God for Winston, whom I used to detest as a political charlatan. He speaks with the voice of the real old England. I'm thrilled to my marrow-bones."

Edward laughed.

"I'll say he's a spell-binder. I am American but I come of English stock, and that guy Churchill makes me want to remember it."

"Put it there, old man," said Hardy, taking his right hand from under the coverlet and holding it out to Edward Hambledon.

Edward shook hands with him, but not with a hard grip. Hardy was still weak after his operation and loss of blood. But he looked young and even boyish now that he was shaved. It was Edward who shaved him every morning with a safety razor borrowed from Armand de Rollencourt. In a pair of blue silk pyjamas, also borrowed from this French officer, he was ready to receive visitors after eleven o'clock, and he was not left in solitude.

Madame de Rollencourt came to tidy his room and rearrange his pillows and always blushed a little when he took her hand and put it to his lips, half-seriously and half in fun.

"You are spoiling me," he told her. "It is worth losing my leg to have so much kindness."

"You do not pay attention to anything I say," replied Madame de Rollencourt. "Have I not told you that it's very naughty to smoke so many cigarettes in your present state of health?"

"On the contrary," answered Hardy, "they soothe my nerves and sustain my morale. Pass me that little packet, *chère madame*."

She laughed, and passed him a packet of *Petits Caporals* which Madeleine had bought for him in Tours.

"You are incorrigible, *mon capitaine*," said Madame de Rollencourt, smoothing down his silk coverlet.

"And you are too good," he told her. "That's what worries me more than anything. What is going to happen to you all if the Boches come and find you harbouring an English officer?"

Madame de Rollencourt hid from him a little anxiety in her eyes. She had discussed this matter with Armand and Edward Hambledon. There was certainly a grave danger. She could not disguise that from herself. For Lucile's sake, especially, she was anxious.

"We shall have to pass you off as our gardener," she answered. "You will have to put on your dirty old clothes again and give up shaving for three mornings a week. That will annoy Madeleine Delaroche, who likes to see you beautiful and debonair."

Hardy laughed and coloured up slightly.

"Mademoiselle Delaroche is charming," he said. "But I don't deserve so much attention."

Mademoiselle Delaroche appeared on the scene again that afternoon. She brought a bouquet of deep red roses and three razor blades which she had bought in Tours, and *L'île des Pingouins*, by Anatole France.

"How goes it, *mon capitaine?*" she asked, standing by his bed.

"Marvellously!" he told her. "As soon as I get my artificial leg I shall be hopping about like a cock robin. Meanwhile, I shall have to get about on crutches."

There was one member of the household who never came to his room. It was Lucile's aunt, Mademoiselle Duchesne. This pale-faced lady in black did not approve of harbouring an English officer. She did not approve of the English. She had made a little scene in the drawing-room downstairs when the news had come that the British Fleet had fired at Darlan's ships in the harbour of Mers el Kebir.

"Did I not tell you?" she cried. "The English are our enemies. They are worse than the Germans, because they pretend to be our friends. They are essentially treacherous. They have no sense of honour or of decency. Always they have betrayed us."

Armand rebuked her severely.

"My dear aunt, you are talking nonsense, as you do every time you speak about these things. England is supporting General de Gaulle and receiving all who can escape from France. It is only with the aid of Britain and her great Empire that France will regain her liberty."

"You are mad, Armand!" said Mademoiselle Duchesne. "Your mother is mad! Lucile is mad! I find this situation intolerable. When the Germans arrive we shall all be shot because of that Englishman upstairs. Is he not well enough to leave us? Does he not know that he is endangering us all? Has he any sense of honour beyond that of his countrymen? Obviously it is not so."

"You are absurd my dear Marie-Claire," said Madame de Rollencourt. "Do you expect him to walk away on one leg? The poor boy is very weak. Apart from your dislike of the English, it is surely necessary to remember that you are a Christian, and a good Catholic."

"I am a good Frenchwoman," answered Mademoiselle Duchesne, tightening her lips. "The English are our hereditary enemies. I hope I have some of the spirit of Jeanne d'Arc, who chased them out of France."

Armand, her nephew, laughed harshly.

"It was we who burnt her as a witch," he said. "In any case, my dear aunt, you are as much unlike Jeanne d'Arc as anyone in the world. She had a sense of humour."

Mademoiselle Duchesne revealed her anger by a sudden flash of colour.

"You insult me, Armand. You are all unkind to me. You all hate me."

Lucile went swiftly across the room and put her arm round her aunt's shoulder and kissed her pale cheek.

"That is very untrue, dear Aunt," she said.

"I had no intention of insulting you," said Armand. "I was only stating an historical fact."

He laughed uneasily when Mademoiselle Duchesne burst into tears and left the room.

XVIII

ARMAND DE ROLLENCOURT was the first to leave the farmhouse of Grancourt Notre-Dame. He had made up his mind to join the army of liberation under General de Gaulle in England, and he was aware that the quicker he went the better his chance of escape. By the terms of the armistice and the line drawn between occupied and unoccupied France the village of Grancourt was fifteen kilometres on the wrong side of the line. Already German soldiers and S.S. men had appeared in neighbouring towns and villages to guard the boundary between the two zones. At any moment they might come to Grancourt Notre-Dame and take up quarters in the farmhouse.

"I must go," said Armand, one night. "I must go at dawn tomorrow. I shall make for the Pyrénées and get through Spain and Portugal. There is already a system. I hear from friends in Tours—François Doumergue—that the system is already well organized. They arrange the necessary visas. They have the rubber stamps and the passport forms printed on a secret press. With a little luck and a little bribery one may pass the frontier. Already many young Frenchmen have reached England that way. Francois Doumergue is their agent in Tours. He is linked up with others in Paris, Bordeaux, Marseilles, and elsewhere. It is their response to the appeal of de Gaulle."

"I know François Doumergue," said Lucile. "He once was foolish enough to fall in love with me. That was when he was sixteen and I was fourteen."

She laughed at this remembrance of a boy and girl love-affair, and then added serious words:

"I should like to be of use to his system."

"He needs an American who can move freely about France without suspicion," answered Armand. "He wishes to meet our good friend here."

Hambledon raised his eyebrows and smiled.

"A risky job, I guess."

Armand de Rollencourt nodded.

"Not without risk," he agreed.

He looked into Hambledon's eyes and smiled as though assured that this American would not shirk the risk.

"He would be grateful if you would call on him one day and have a talk," he added. "He is editor of *La Gazette de Tours*. You will find him a charming young man, though very delicate and unfit for military service."

"I shall be glad to meet him," answered Edward.

That night Armand said farewell to Kit Hardy.

"I'm leaving at dawn," he said. "I hope to be in England before many weeks have passed."

For a moment Hardy was upset by emotion.

"Oh, Christ!" he said, as a kind of prayer. "If only I could come with you. I would give my right arm as well as my right leg."

"You will follow on," answered Armand, much moved by this cry of anguish. "As soon as you are able to move about, my friend."

"I lie here like a useless log," said Hardy, deeply distressed.

For a moment there were tears in his eyes or something very like them. For a moment he put his head under the bed-clothes like a boy ashamed of tears.

Armand patted his shoulder and spoke in a kindly voice:

"My dear fellow, I know how you feel. I shall feel like that when I am in exile from France."

Presently Hardy flung back the bed-clothes and sat up.

"Give my love to England," he said. "Tell my family that I hang on to the English broadcasts for every scrap of news and that I think of them always. Tell them that I think the R.A.F. is beyond words splendid and wonderful, and that one day I'm going to join it with a wooden leg."

"I will deliver your letters," said Armand, who seemed sure of getting to England.

The letters were already written. They were already in Armand's breast-pocket.

"My mother will be delighted to meet you," said Hardy. "I am green with envy of you, old man. Tell her that I am grateful to your own mother, who risks her life for my sake."

He held out his left hand in the French style and Armand gripped it for a moment and then swung on his heel and left the room.

With Edward that night he spoke a few serious words.

"I feel that I am leaving my best friend behind. I am less anxious about my mother and sister, knowing that you are here to protect them for a while. I have perfect faith in you, my friend, both in your kindness and in your courage."

"I will try not to disappoint you," said Edward lightly, shy of French emotionalism.

"I am cycling to Tours," said Armand. "I shall set out before the light of day. I have to pass the barriers between the two zones. I shall only get my *sauf conduit* when I reach Tours, where François Doumergue has one waiting for me. I shall have to dodge the patrols; but I know every hedge in this countryside and I shall get through all right."

"Take care of yourself," said Edward.

"*Mon cher Edouard,*" said Armand. "I will not say *Adieu*, but *Au revoir*. One day we shall meet again."

He held out his arms, embraced Edward warmly, and kissed him on both cheeks.

"Say, you make me blush!" said Edward. "We don't do that in the United States. No, sir!"

Armand laughed and raised his hand.

"*Bonne chance, mon ami.*"

He went away from Edward's room. It was late at night, but Madame de Rollencourt and Lucile were still sitting up to see the last of Armand. The murmur of their voices came up to Hambledon's room where he sat reading a book. Presently they were silent. Edward heard bolts being drawn in the hall and felt a little draught come under his own door as the front door was opened. It was not yet dawn, but Armand was setting out on his adventure.

A few minutes later footsteps passed Edward's room. A woman was weeping. It was Madame de Rollencourt, that gracious lady.

A girl's voice spoke aloud. It was Lucile.

"*Courage, maman!*"

XIX

THE GERMANS CAME to Granville.

The Rollencourts' old gardener-farmhand, Gaston, was first to bring the news.

"They have arrived!" he said, standing in the doorway of the breakfast-room at eight o'clock one morning.

There was no need to ask who "they" were.

Madame de Rollencourt, who was pouring out coffee, spilt some and put the pot down with an unsteady hand.

Lucile, who was in a blue silk dressing-gown, looked at Edward across the table and he saw the distress in her eyes.

Mademoiselle Duchesne was the first to speak.

"It was, of course, inevitable."

She also looked at Edward and spoke to him coldly.

"Our lives are in danger, *m'sieur*, so long as that English officer is upstairs. When do you take him away? Perhaps it is too late even now. In that case, you are responsible for what happens."

Madame de Rollencourt answered her sharply.

"I am responsible, Marie-Claire. This is my house. Our English friend is my guest."

Mademoiselle Duchesne looked at her sister angrily, and little lines deepened about her eyes and mouth.

"I am, of course, a pauper. You do not let me forget. I live on your charity, Louise. But as your sister I have a right to speak, and I now remind you that it is a crime punishable by death to harbour English prisoners of war who have escaped. Do you not think of Lucile? Do you wish to be shot against your garden wall? Are you utterly careless of *my* life?"

Madame de Rollencourt continued to pour out the coffee, though her hand still trembled slightly, as Edward noticed.

"We have thought it all out," she answered. "Captain Hardy has already been moved to the cottage next to that of Gaston. His papers are in perfect order. He is now Pierre Prunier. Please remember that."

"It is idiotic," cried Mademoiselle Duchesne in a shrill voice. "Everyone here knows that he is not Pierre Prunier. Gaston knows; his wife knows. The two maids know—Suzanne and Nanette. Their families know. Do you think that secret can be kept from the Germans? In any case, will they not suspect a man who has lost his leg and looks like an Englishman and speaks with a foreign accent? How did this man lose his leg? they will ask."

"We have our answer ready," answered Madame de Rollencourt. "It was the result of a German bomb which fell in Grancourt."

Lucile spoke to her aunt good-naturedly, but Edward noticed that her hand was also shaky when she passed him a roll of bread.

"You see, Aunt Marie-Claire, that we have thought out everything. Or rather, we have had the good advice of our friend *Monsieur* Hambledon, who is very intelligent."

Her eyes smiled across the table to Edward.

"I thank you, lady," he said, returning her smile, though at the back of his mind there was a sense of uneasiness because "they" had arrived in Grancourt Notre-Dame.

According to Gaston, who had departed before the family altercation, there were only about a dozen of them who had come with two officers in a military truck. The men had gone into the Reine Jeanne and were drinking French beer. They had smiled at the inhabitants and seemed civil enough. They were like young peasant boys, tanned by the sun and blue-eyed.

It was in the afternoon that the farmhouse was visited by the two German officers. One of the maids—Nanette—came into the drawing-room to announce them. She was white to the lips and could hardly speak.

"Two Germans . . . Officers . . . They wish to speak with Madame."

Coffee had been served, and Edward was there with Madame de Rollencourt and Lucile.

"Must I see them?" asked Madame de Rollencourt in a low voice to Edward.

"I think so," he answered.

"Ask them to come in, Nanette," said Madame de Rollencourt.

Two young men entered the drawing-room and bowed as they stood inside the door. Edward's eyes were fixed upon them with such a scrutiny that he could have drawn their portraits afterwards, at least in caricature. One was a tall, thin young man with a student's face, not typically German, but dark, with deep-set eyes behind horn-rimmed glasses, and a lean-sharp-featured face. The other was more Teutonic, with fair hair, cut very short, and blue eyes.

"Pardon us for this intrusion, *mesdames*," said the dark young man in very good French. He seemed nervous and embarrassed. The fair young man glanced round the room with a smile and his eyes came to rest on Lucile for more than an instant.

Madame de Rollencourt and Lucile had risen from their chairs, so that Edward stood up also, though he had intended to remain seated.

"What is it you wish, gentlemen?" asked Madame de Rollencourt with cold dignity.

"You will excuse us, I hope," said the dark young man, "but we have orders to occupy the village of Grancourt Notre-Dame, which is not far from the border between Occupied and Unoccupied France, as doubtless you know. My friend and I belong to the Boundary Commission. It will be our duty to maintain the regulations laid down regarding the prohibition of traffic and intercourse between the two zones."

"Yes?" asked Madame de Rollencourt, as though she were not interested in all this and did not see how it applied to her.

"Doubtless we shall be here for some length of time," said the dark young man. For a moment he smiled and then added a few words which were not amusing.

"That may depend perhaps on the duration of the war."

"Yes?" asked Madame de Rollencourt.

"My orders," said the young German, "are to secure billets for myself and my brother officer in this farmhouse. I should regret if that gives you any annoyance as an intrusion upon your private life."

Madame de Rollencourt answered him in her glacial voice.

"It is, of course, an intrusion which I have no power to resist."

The dark young man flushed slightly and then spoke politely with a faint smile.

"We shall behave very correctly, madame, I assure you. We have very simple needs. Perhaps you will be able to provide breakfast and an evening meal and two small rooms upstairs. You will permit us to see your bedrooms for two moments?"

"When you like," answered the lady.

The young man bowed stiffly.

They played games together like a boy and girl. There was a French version of Snap which amused them very much and caused Madeleine to squeal with laughter, because of Hardy's talented imitation of cocks crowing, and pigs grunting, and donkeys hee-haw-ing, with other farmyard animals. Madeleine taught him an elaborate version of Patience, and he accused her of cheating when she substituted one card for another because things wouldn't work out according to plan.

"*Il faut faire une petite supposition,*" she answered on those occasions.

"Tell me about the two Boches," he asked from time to time. "How are they behaving? Has that young blond beast made abominable overtures to Nanette or Suzanne?"

Madeleine had nothing good to say of Karl Schwarzwald.

"He is intolerable! I find his eyes always following me about. If I look at him by accident he smiles with a mixture of boldness and shyness."

"I can't help being sorry for the young swine," said Hardy. "You are a very attractive young lady. All Germans are romantic when they are not torturing Jews or shooting hostages. He is, no doubt, desperately in love with you. That is very natural."

"I find it disgusting," answered Madeleine. "God be praised, I have never given him a civil word. When I pass him on the stairs and he stands on one side with exaggerated courtesy I pass him like a ghost."

"What about the other one?" asked Hardy. "Hambledon tells me that he is intellectual and very anxious to be friendly."

"He is a better type," admitted Madeleine. "For a German he is not entirely horrible."

Hardy laughed at this qualified praise.

"Some of them are fairly decent," he said. "If they could get rid of Hitler and free themselves from the spell he is putting upon them I've no doubt most of them would be quite sensible. I found them so when I had a holiday in Germany before the war."

"That is the English point of view!" cried Madeleine. "It is why we have this second war. You English have no sense of hatred for the Germans. You forget all their crimes. You think that they may be melted by kindness and converted by reason. You think that, naturally, they are like other people. We French know that this is wrong. The Germans have different shaped heads. They were never really touched by Latin civilization. They remain the outer barbarians—the Vandals and the Goths."

They had a little argument about this, fierce on the part of Madeleine until he made her laugh.

"Are we quarrelling, by any chance? If so, I surrender."

He held up both hands and said: "*Kamerad*!"

One evening, many weeks later, he asked her with a glint in his eyes whether she would do him a particular favour which would greatly improve his moral well-being.

"Is it something ridiculous?" asked Madeleine suspiciously, because of that glint in his eyes. "What is it you wish me to do?"

Hardy answered with sham diffidence.

"I don't know whether this little favour is in accordance with French tradition. Perhaps I had better not mention it."

"Tell me!" pleaded Madeleine. "In any case, I must go before ten minutes have passed. I am like Cinderella at the ball. Only I have to flee before seven o'clock when those two Boches come back."

"It's just a kiss I want," said Hardy. "It wouldn't take long and it would do me a power of good."

Madeleine listened to his request with her head turned away from him, and a little smile about her lips, and a flush of colour creeping up from her neck.

"Is it in accordance with English tradition?" she asked.

"It is," he assured her. "But I am anxious about French habits and customs."

"Such things are not unknown in France," answered Madeleine. "Young women have been known to kiss young men. Young men have not entirely neglected the impulse of love and nature. In fact, I may say French literature is rather candid about that."

Hardy laughed at the nonsense they were both talking and held out his arms as he lay there in bed with only one leg beneath the sheets.

She went down on her knees by the bedside and lowered her head and let him kiss her on her lips, and inside her ears, and on her closed eyes, and under her chin. They were very nice kisses for an Englishman, she thought.

She fled from him as the clock gave a kind of shudder and then struck seven times.

XXI

HARDY WAS IN touch with the outer world by means of a little box installed in his room by Hambledon. Over the microphone he listened to the B.B.C. and did not like what he heard during those autumn months when he still stayed in hiding, unable to move from his truckle-bed.

He agonized because of the Blitz over England, agonized over the destruction of ancient shrines and the slaughter of civilians, but marvelled at the courage and endurance of his own people. There were times when he laughed at the description of life in the shelters and the unbeatable sense of humour of those who had been bombed out of their homes and shops.

"It's miraculous, Edward, old man," he said to Hambledon one day.

"What is?" asked Edward. "I'm not sure that I believe in miracles, and I'm not sure that I don't!"

"The spirit of the English people," said Hardy. "It's supernatural. It's more than human nature ought to be asked to stand; but, by God, they're standing it—the Cockneys—God bless 'em—my crowd, and the people of Coventry, and Birmingham, and Portsmouth, and all the other cities which these swine are bombing to dust and ashes."

"It's pretty wonderful," agreed Hambledon. "I wonder if my people could stand up to it as well. I'm not sure about that."

Every time some historical place had been hit, and was revealed later by the censorship, Hardy groaned in mental anguish.

"The Guildhall . . . how frightful! . . . Temple Church . . . Damn and blast them! . . . St. Paul's . . . Oh, God! Oh, God!"

Hambledon tried to comfort him.

"Those ancient monuments can be rebuilt. I'm more sorry for the massacre of the innocents."

One afternoon Hardy sat up in bed and spoke earnestly.

"This war against civilians is worse than anything in history. What are we going to do about it, Hambledon?"

"Meaning you and me?" asked Hambledon, with his quiet smile.

"Meaning all of us," answered Hardy. "Meaning humanity as a whole. The bombing aeroplane is destroying all moralities. We're fighting a war without pity on women and children, without regard for all the things that have been built up by centuries of civilization. We're going down into a black abyss of scientific barbarism. Shall we ever climb out again or will the next war be worse than this, or the end of this war worse than the beginning? Isn't it the suicide of civilization?"

"I'll say it is," answered Hambledon. "On the other hand, we've got to smash this evil spirit let loose by Hitler. He can't be allowed to get away with it."

"Not on your life!" said Hardy. "But it's a horrible dilemma. It's a competition in mass murder. We shall have to use the enemy's methods and go one better in order to beat him. I see that. For one bomb he sends over now we shall send over a hundred one day if he gives us time. Every German city will be a mass of rubble. And so far have I departed from my beautiful little ideals that I gloat over the thought of that day coming."

He asked an abrupt question.

"Are you Americans coming in with your men as well as your machines?"

"You bet we are," answered Hambledon. "It's going to work out that way. Roosevelt is leading us forward to that goal. But it takes time. We shall be more than a bit late again."

On another afternoon he found Hardy restless in mind and body.

"Ned," he said, "you must get me out of this. I must get back to England before I go *gaga*. I lie here like a stuck pig."

"Doesn't Madeleine relieve your boredom?" asked Hambledon with a smile.

Hardy gave a laugh.

"She does! I'm devoted to her. She makes this place a paradise, but I feel guilty about it. While other men are dying I'm having a love idyll. While English people are being slaughtered in mean streets I lie here with love in idleness. Not too good, old man!"

Hambledon laughed at this sense of guilt.

"I shouldn't quarrel with your luck. You've paid for it. You've lost one good leg in the service of your country. Isn't that enough?"

Hardy was doubtful about that.

XXII

As AN AMERICAN and a student of human nature Hambledon did not avoid all conversation with the two Germans billeted in the farmhouse. Lucile reproached him for getting on too friendly terms with them and was not convinced by his argument that it was interesting to study German psychology, and that, anyhow, it might be useful later on if he disarmed their suspicions and gained their good will.

"Helmuth Winter," he told her, "is a good type. I like him."

"No German is a good type," said Lucile, "and it is very wrong of you to like him."

"He is a civilized human being," said Hambledon. "He has no real allegiance to the Nazi creed. He hates war. He is an artist with an artist's outlook on life."

"Nevertheless," answered Lucile, "he obeys Hitler, and is an enemy of France and all civilized nations."

Hambledon smiled into her eyes.

"I don't expect you to be tolerant, and I don't want you to accuse me of being pro-German, but it's fair to say on behalf of one German that he has a deep admiration for French civilization—its history and literature—and has no enmity whatever against the French people."

"He tells you so," answered Lucile with cold scepticism. "It is just German propaganda dictated by that wretch Goebbels to deceive and weaken us into cowardly collaboration."

Edward laughed and shook his head.

"I believe in his sincerity. He takes a risk in talking to me as he does."

"*Edouard!*" cried Lucile in a troubled voice, "do not make friends with our enemies."

It was difficult to be unfriendly with Helmuth Winter. He had a certain charm of manner. One evening he had tapped at Edward's door and asked him whether he would care to see some water-colour sketches he had done of the French countryside.

"I certainly would," answered Edward.

The sketches were excellent and Edward admired his technique. They talked for a while about art and the young German officer expressed his admiration for the French impressionists.

Presently he gave a little sigh.

"This war spoils all that!" he exclaimed. "It is the enemy of all art."

Edward agreed whole-heartedly.

"Why did you people make this war?" he asked with his American candour.

Helmuth Winter raised his hands slightly.

"The German people did not make it. The Führer assured them a thousand times that he stood for peace. They believed him."

"But they followed him when he made war," answered Edward.

The German lieutenant shrugged his shoulders slightly.

"All people obey the call when their country goes to war. Reason is dethroned. My country right or wrong! Before the war I was in Munich. I was there when the English Chamberlain came with his umbrella. Thousands of Germans, thousands of mothers and fathers came out to cheer him as a messenger of peace. German women lay down on the railway lines to prevent the troop trains taking away their sons to the front. There are many Germans in concentration camps because they spoke against war."

"Now they rejoice in German victories," answered Edward. "They think Hitler is a miracle worker. Don't they worship him?"

Helmuth Winter lowered his voice.

"There are many who do not rejoice even in German victories. There is a saying among them: '*Wir siegen uns todt.*' We are winning ourselves to death. There are no cheers when the troops march through Berlin or Munich. Only the young idiots stuffed with the Nazi creed—the preposterous nonsense of *Mein Kampf*—the poisonous philosophy of Rosenberg—make a god of Hitler and follow him blindly, even if death is at the end of the road. I am not one of those. I believe in peace; I believe in beauty. I look upon this war as a devilish evil, though we are not alone to blame for it. Hitler was born out of German misery after Versailles, and the unpayable reparations which destroyed the mark, and caused a tide of unemployment. As a boy I remember those days. My parents nearly went mad."

He went on talking in a monologue.

"This war, of course, is the failure of Christianity and of human comradeship. The Christian churches line themselves up with their nation's interests. This war and the last were a denial of Christ's teaching. Germany is not alone in its violation of the Christian spirit. In the past as well as now. The present and all its horrors have been born out of the past."

He laughed suddenly and apologized.

"Forgive me for talking like this. It is very boring for you."

"I'm interested," answered Edward. "I agree with you to some extent."

"Karl Schwarzwald," said Winter with a smile, "would denounce me as a traitor if he heard me say these things. He is a simple boy and his head is stuffed with Nazi ideas about the *Herrenvolk* and German destiny to world power. We cannot talk reasonably together."

Before Edward left his room he expressed his thanks for the conversation.

"I have an intellectual hunger for a little intelligent talk. It is very difficult to break down the hostility of the French people. They answer in monosyllables. When I go into a café in Tours they do not even look at me. Even Karl Schwarzwald finds that intolerable. In Munich, when he entered a café, the girls' eyes brightened because of his youth and good looks. Now the French girls turn their eyes away or change their chairs if he sits near them. It is very trying for a young man with self-conceit and an adolescent desire for female companionship!"

Lieutenant Winter smiled at this psycho-analysis of his brother officer. Then he changed the subject abruptly.

"One day I should much like to see some of your own work."

"I will show you some sketches I have done of Mademoiselle de Rollencourt," said Edward.

"That would be a great favour," answered the German officer warmly. "A thousand thanks."

It was on another evening, later in history, that he gave a piece of news to Edward which was also perhaps a friendly warning.

"I hear that some S.S. men are arriving tomorrow to check up on all persons in the village of Grancourt Notre-Dame. No doubt they will come here and will wish to see everyone's *carte d'identité* and other papers."

"That's all right with me," answered Edward calmly.

Helmuth Winter nodded and smiled in a friendly way.

"Oh, of course. But I thought you might like to know."

It was useful to know, mainly because of Christopher Hardy, who was now walking around on crutches brought over by Dr. Moineau in his dilapidated little car, for which he could still obtain a certain amount of "juice," as he called it. But in the clothes he was now wearing he would not pass as a peasant. He went about in one of Armand's sky-blue polo shirts and in a pair of flannel trousers. Certainly he would not pass as Pierre Prunier the gardener.

Then there was the question of his *carte d'identité.* Would that pass the careful examination of S.S. men? Hambledon had tinkered about with it considerably. With Lucile's camera he had taken a photograph of Hardy, unshaven after four days, and had substituted this for the face of Pierre Prunier, a typical French peasant with a much-lined face. The trouble had been about the rubber stamp which had covered a corner of the photograph. It had been necessary to reproduce that missing part and Edward had spent several days of careful artistry on that delicate job. He had drawn the stamp on a piece of linoleum and cut it out with a razor edge. After many failures he had succeeded fairly well. Lucile had declared it to be a masterpiece, and he was almost satisfied. There was only one little bit which was not a hundred-per-cent. perfect. It was where his razor had slipped in cutting the linoleum. It had blurred the green ink slightly.

Before the S.S. men arrived Hardy—thanks to the tip from Helmuth Winter—had put on a ragged shirt and a pair of old weather-stained trousers. He had omitted to shave that morning and had smudged his face with a touch of grease.

"*Qui êtes vous?*" asked one of the S.S. men in a harsh German accent.

"*Pierre Prunier, jardinier.*"

"*Votre carte d'identité.*"

Hardy produced his faked card. The S.S. man examined it minutely and then handed it back.

"*Ça va.*"

Edward's careful work had passed. It was all right. His own American passport had been handed back politely and the S.S. man had spoken a few words in English.

"We have no quarrel with the Americans."

"That is good."

"May I ask why are you staying here?"

"I am a friend of the family."

"I understand."

He smiled and glanced towards Lucile, who was in the sitting-room during this interrogation of the family and servants. His smile and glance clearly meant that he saw a good reason for Edward staying with this French family.

"*A votre service!*"

He saluted smartly in the Fascist style.

"*Heil Hitler!*"

"Good afternoon," answered Edward, with fair civility.

They waited until the two S.S. men were well away and then laughed.

"It was marvellous!" cried Lucile. "Your artist's work deceived them utterly. What one can do once, one can do twice, and a hundred times! We must set up a factory for false passports."

"Hush!" said Madame de Rollencourt, who had been very nervous when the S.S. men had arrived.

Mademoiselle Duchesne came into the room which she had left only a few moments before.

"Why do you say 'Hush'?" she asked suspiciously. "Are you talking secrets which you do not wish me to hear?"

"Which I do not wish the servants to hear," answered Madame de Rollencourt, quietly. "It was something about our gardener, Pierre Prunier."

Mademoiselle Duchesne crossed herself.

"God have mercy on us!" she cried. "Our lives are not safe for a moment as long as that man stays here. You are all mad. I have said so before. Now Madeleine has fallen in love with him and stays with him alone in his bedroom. It is abominable."

It was Lucile who answered angrily.

"Madeleine has been helping to nurse him. Do you find that abominable?"

She did, and Edward Hambledon, who in most of his human contacts was tolerant and good-natured, spoke harsh words in his secret mind.

"I would like to strangle that female! She's as sour as a quince."

XXIII

THE BOIS DES FÉES—the Fairy wood—looked down upon the boundary line between Occupied and Unoccupied France with a view of the broad road lined with poplars where there was the German barrier at which all traffic was stopped, and a hundred yards farther on the French barrier. By avoiding the road, and after a careful watch for German patrols, it was not too difficult to get into Unoccupied France and the city of Tours by field-paths and thickets. Edward Hambledon came to know every yard of this way, and it amused him to dodge the German guards and get across the line. In any case, his American passport and a *sauf-conduit* provided for him by François Doumergue would get him out of trouble if he happened to meet it, but he preferred the secret way in order to avert suspicion if he went through the two barriers on frequent journeys. By that way he had gone to see François Doumergue, who was anxious to meet a helpful American.

This young man, who had escaped military service because of tuberculosis, had a printing and publishing establishment in Tours, and it was in this office that Edward met him. He was a thin, dark young man who looked as if a puff of wind would blow him away because of his slight and delicate build. But inside his frail body there was the flame of an ardent spirit and a courage which was prepared to risk all things for France.

He shook hands warmly with Edward and locked his door before beginning his conversation.

"Armand has spoken to me about you," he said. "I have been deeply anxious to get in touch with you."

"What do you want me to do?" asked Edward. "Something pretty dangerous, I guess."

François Doumergue laughed and shook his head.

"Not too dangerous—with reasonable care—but very helpful to General de Gaulle and those who will never tolerate the surrender by Vichy and those traitors who have betrayed France."

"Tell me," said Edward. "I'm not really keen if it leads to a white wall and a firing squad."

François Doumergue smiled and flicked off the ash of his cigarette.

"Oh, well, that may happen to some of us, but it's very unlikely in your case. Behind you is the power of the United States, which looks after its citizens. Let me explain a little."

He explained quite a lot. Friends of his in Paris and elsewhere were organizing the way of escape for men of military age and fighting spirit.

They were collecting passports from dead soldiers which would need a little alteration and a change of photographs. They would like to get hold of Vichy passports for reproduction.

"I have a very good printing press," he said with a smile, "and some very skilful compositors. We could reproduce quite perfectly any passports and other official documents permitting individuals to leave France for North Africa and Portugal. But we must first get those documents."

Hambledon smiled, with that slow smile which twisted his lips and lit up his eyes.

"Not so easy," he remarked.

"There is always a way," answered Doumergue with quiet confidence.

Another part of the plan was to keep in touch with friends who could raise money. Escape was sometimes a costly affair for young men who had no funds of their own.

"Correspondence is forbidden between the two zones," he explained. "And, in any case, written letters are subject to examination by the Gestapo and the Vichy police. I have here the addresses of two or three people in Vichy and Paris with whom I wish to communicate urgently. If you would be good enough to hand them a few documents and bring back their answers it would be a great service. Another matter! I understand from Armand that Madame de Rollencourt and Mademoiselle Lucile are willing to harbour escaped prisoners of war and others for a night or two now and then and to guide them across the boundary by way of the Bois des Fées."

"There are two Germans in Madame de Rollencourt's house," answered Edward. "Isn't that like walking into a trap?"

"They wouldn't enter the house itself," answered Doumergue. "They would go to the cottage now inhabited by Pierre Prunier and then make their way to the Bois des Fées. They would need food and guidance."

Hambledon stared down at the polished floor-boards under his feet. Presently he raised his head and spoke gravely:

"I'm prepared to take a bit of a risk," he said. "It might be amusing; but I don't agree with endangering the life of a young girl like Mademoiselle de Rollencourt. I'm against that."

François Doumergue was not against that.

"She is eager to take the risk," he said. "She is not alone among French women and young girls who are ready and eager to join the secret ranks behind General de Gaulle. But we will take every care that Mademoiselle Lucile will not come to any harm. The risk is very slight, I think. It will be less when your friend Captain Hardy gets away from Grancourt. Madame and Mademoiselle de Rollencourt have not shirked that danger in which I understand you acquiesced."

Edward nodded.

"He had a leg lopped off. He couldn't get away. But I agree—the sooner the better."

"It is one reason why I wish to see you," explained Doumergue.

"We have arranged for his passage from Marseilles to North Africa. We have very good relations in Marseilles. They are in close touch with the owners of merchant ships who are still getting across the Mediterranean. Is it possible for your friend to leave by next Friday?"

"He will make it possible," answered Edward. "If he has to walk all the way."

Doumergue smiled. "He won't have to walk. We shall send him down by train. A young lady will go with him. For the time being she will be his sister. We have already made out her papers accordingly."

"Fine work!" exclaimed Edward, with enthusiasm for efficiency.

"He should come to the Bois des Fées at dawn on Friday," said Doumergue. "With care he may get across the boundary when the guard changes. Doubtless you will see to that."

"I certainly will."

Before he left the printing office he made a half-promise.

"I may take a trip to Vichy and Paris. If so, I'll get in touch with your friends."

"A thousand thanks, my dear sir. You are a good friend of France. Armand told me so, and you have a generous heart. That also he told me."

Hambledon answered modestly with a good-natured laugh.

"A kind heart but a soft head."

That evening he conveyed the news to Christopher Hardy, who was in the cottage reading a French novel, with his crutches propped up against a chair.

Edward grinned at him.

"Care to go to England?" he asked, casually.

Hardy looked up from his book with a quizzical smile.

"Trying to pull my leg?"

"Next Friday morning at dawn," said Edward. "It's all arranged, *via* Marseilles and North Africa."

"A fairy-tale?" asked Hardy, incredulously, and yet excited.

"God's own truth," answered Hardy. "How do you feel about it, Kit?"

Christopher Hardy did not tell him all that he felt about it. He did not tell him that he was torn in half by this news. In half his brain and half his heart his thoughts leapt towards England, to be among his own folk again, to see his father and mother, to share the ordeal of war with them, to get going again, somehow. In half his brain and half his heart he hated to leave this cottage because of a girl who had given him her love and made it paradise for him. Madeleine and he had had happy hours here, laughing a lot because he made her laugh, playing childish games because in spirit they were still very young, arguing, quarrelling, and making love ardently and without boredom on either side. It would be hard to say good-bye to Madeleine.

She found it hard to say good-bye to him. She came down to the cottage in the darkness of that Thursday evening before he went at dawn next morning. He heard her at the door—the four little taps they had arranged as their secret code—and hobbled across the room to let her in. She stood there in a raincoat with a hood which came over her head. She was carrying a lantern which she shaded with her hand.

"*Christophe!*" she whispered. "This is our last night. It is terrible."

"I feel like death about it," he told her, "and yet I know it's not death. I shall see you again. I shall come back."

He led her into the room and took off her raincloak and flung it to the floor and then put his arms about her.

"My very dear Madeleine! My well beloved! My fairy from the Bois des Fées. How can I leave you?"

His French was very perfect now. He had learnt a lot from Madeleine.

"I shall die without you, *Christophe*," she answered with a sob.

"No! No! Time will pass like a flash of lightning. I'll come back on wings. I shall learn to fly. One leg is as good as two in the air."

"I shall be an old woman before you come back," said Madeleine, in a despairing voice. "This war is going on for years and years. Hitler is now winning in Russia. How can we ever beat Germany?"

"We shall beat them," answered Hardy. "England always wins the last battle. Somehow, by some kind of miracle, we shall beat them in the end."

"*Christophe mon chéri!*" cried Madeleine.

He held her very close in his arms. He kissed her with the passion of a man who says good-bye to love.

"Do not go!" cried Madeleine. "Stay here always. Is not my love enough for you? Is England more to you than I am?"

Christopher Hardy groaned with the agony of this temptation. Why should he go? He had lost a limb for England. He had done his bit. Why not stay with his love?

"I must go," he told her after that inward struggle. "If I stayed much longer I should be discovered and bring grave trouble upon you all. I must get back to England and share the sufferings of my own people."

"Then I shall never see you again," cried Madeleine. "You will be bombed to death in London, or drowned before you get there. I shall be left alone to weep out my eyes."

Hardy laughed at her, but with an ache in his heart.

"I was born under a lucky star," he told her. "That star brought me here. It will bring me here again. Let me kiss you once more, little Madeleine."

But he did not kiss her that time. He held her in a hard grip and listened intently.

"Someone is coming down the path," he said. "It's a man. But Edward never comes as late as this and is going to meet me at dawn."

He held her tight and pushed her into the little kitchen as both of them heard a cough and then a knock at the door at the end of a stick.

"Be very quiet," whispered Hardy. "Do not move."

He went to the door and opened it.

"*Qui va la?*"

It was the figure of a man in German uniform. It was Karl Schwarzwald, whom he had seen several times while he was working in the garden.

"It is raining like the devil," said Schwarzwald in his harsh French. "I will come in until the storm is passed."

Without with your leave or by your leave he strode into the cottage and took out his handkerchief to wipe the rain from his tunic.

"I did not take my cape this morning," he said. "It was a foolish mistake."

"The autumn rains begin," said Hardy.

Schwarzwald nodded and glanced round the room. He saw the novel which Hardy had been reading, and picked it up.

"You read the novels of Marcel Proust?" he asked. "As a gardener you choose difficult books!"

"No, no!" answered Hardy, detecting a note of suspicion. "It was one of the young ladies of the house who left it here by mistake. I do not read novels by Marcel Proust or anyone else. I have my work to do."

Schwarzwald smiled and lit a cigarette which he took from a silver case.

"I thought it strange," he admitted. He sat down in Hardy's armchair with its horse-hair seat and curved arms. Then he yawned loudly.

"It is very boring, this life," he said. "I die of boredom. You call it *le cafard*, do you not? It is a dreadful malady."

"I have suffered from it," said Hardy. "After my leg was amputated."

Schwarzwald stretched out his two legs and gave another yawn.

"A pretty girl would help matters," he said. "But there are no pretty girls except those two at the house who are very proud and cold. I understand, of course. It is because I am German and therefore in their minds an enemy. All the same, it is unpleasant."

Hardy did not feel called upon to answer this. He was thinking of Madeleine only a yard or so away in the darkness of the kitchen.

Schwarzwald talked for a few minutes about the weather and the countryside. He seemed to talk more to hear his own voice than to hold conversation with Pierre Prunier. Suddenly he rose and went to a deal table where Hardy kept his tobacco pouch, long since empty.

"I like that," said Schwarzwald. "It is what I want. How much will you take for it?"

"I do not sell it," answered Hardy.

It had been given to him by his father.

Schwarzwald examined it, and saw a name printed on it.

Christopher Hardy.

"How did you come by it?" he asked. "That is an English name." He looked at this young man who called himself Pierre Prunier, and there was suspicion in his eyes again.

"It belonged to an English soldier in the last war," said Hardy. "He gave it to my father on the battlefields of the Somme. That is why I keep it."

"So?"

Schwarzwald seemed to accept this story, but several times Hardy was aware of his eyes staring at him.

It was half an hour before he went away when the rain ceased. To Hardy it had seemed like four hours. He waited until he heard Schwarzwald's heavy tread down the tiled path and then went to the kitchen and whispered:

"Madeleine! You are there?"

She drew a deep breath, and came into the light, blinking.

"That was a horrible experience! It seemed to last for ever. There was a moment when I wanted to sneeze."

Hardy laughed and held up his hands.

"Thank God you didn't. That young swine is already suspicious. He has gone away with a query in his mind which beyond doubt he will pass on to the German police. It is time I left Grancourt Notre-Dame."

"*Christophe!*" cried Madeleine. "Do not go. Or, if you go, tell me a thousand times that you will keep me in your heart as I shall keep you."

He told her so, not a thousand times for lack of time. She wept and he kissed her wet eyes. It was a night of love too short before the dawn which glimmered through the windows.

"It is time, my dearest," said Hardy.

Footsteps sounded down the tiled path.

Hambledon had come to fetch him.

XXIV

VICHY . . . THE TRAGEDY of France had changed its character out of all likeness to its past as a health resort and social rendezvous for French and English visitors who had drunk its water, gambled in its casino, attended the Russian ballet, played tennis—if they were young and vigorous—shot clay pigeons, and lingered long over lunches in luxury hotels or in white villas looking on to flower gardens. No English lords were here now with their ladies. No French politicians came here with their mistresses as an escape from the lobbies of the *Chambre des Deputés*—though some of them were here with their mistresses as an escape from the consequences of German victory. The French Government under Marshal Pétain, had taken over the hotels and the villas. Crowds of minor officials with their families had surged into this place built for delight, and now the dwelling-place of defeat, despair, humiliation, and enforced collaboration with an enemy who had the whip-hand, and the power and will to use it, ruthlessly if need be.

In the cafés and restaurants there was interminable argument in low voices by men uneasy in their consciences or deep in treachery. Among them were secret agents in the pay of Germany, police spies, lickspittles of Laval, who kept closely in touch with the German overlords and played a traitor's game against the old Marshal, who, in the opinion of many Frenchmen, did his best for France with dignity and tact.

To the followers of de Gaulle and to all those who believed that France had been betrayed by the terms of surrender Vichy was the infamous name, the place of shame, the headquarters of cowardice and treachery. They spoke the word Vichy with a passionate contempt. "The men of Vichy" were to them synonymous with all that was vile. Pétain they could only pardon—if at all—by a shrug of the shoulders and the words: "He is *gaga*. He is a poor old man in his dotage." The name of Laval, that little man with a greasy complexion and the soul of a Judas, as they described him, activated their endocrine glands and turned them green with suppressed rage.

To Vichy came Edward Hambledon one day, and people turned now and then to look furtively at this tall, loose-limbed young American—so obviously an American—who glanced about him with a slight smile about his lips as though amused to find himself here. Perhaps they envied him his look of carelessness and detachment. There was nothing morbid in his eyes. He was not haggard and self-tortured like so many here. He strode through the streets with his head up and that little smile about his lips.

"*Un bon type!*" said a French lady to her husband as he passed. A good type, she thought, and certainly an American.

He lunched with Chas Hunt in a little restaurant which seemed to have been appropriated by American journalists.

"Tell me about the set-up here," said Edward. "Has old Pétain any power? Does he think he has any pull with the Boches? Why does the United States back this Vichy puppet-show by keeping its representatives here? Pretty futile, isn't it?"

Hunt had been astonished to see Edward walk into his office. He was inquisitive as to Edward's recent history since that adventure they had had on the roads of Normandy. So far Hambledon had not enlightened him much. Now he was asking difficult questions.

"I came here with a lot of prejudice," said Hunt. "Now I'm watching things with an open mind and it's darned interesting."

Edward laughed over his cigarette.

"Don't tell me you are a faithful follower of Laval. That sewer rat! You can't make me believe that, Chas."

Chas didn't want him to believe it.

"I'd like to see him guillotined in the Place de la Concorde—one day he will be. But old Pétain is different. He has the respect of most Frenchmen and he's playing a crafty game with Hitler, who is afraid of pushing him too far. Pétain has two trump cards in his hand and Hitler knows it."

"What are they?" asked Edward, with deep scepticism.

"The French Fleet and North Africa. Pétain has the allegiance of those in North Africa. It would be bad for Hitler if they went over to the other side. Same with the Fleet, which Hitler's hands itch to grab."

"I'm for de Gaulle," said Edward, squarely. "I'm for the French policy of resistance. That's in the heroic tradition of France."

Chas Hunt looked at him in a scrutinizing way.

"Say, Edward," he said, "don't forget you're an American citizen. Don't put your head into a noose by getting mixed up with this sabotage stuff, or any part of the underground movement. It's too damn dangerous."

"We'll talk about that later," said Edward. "This place is too public and there's an ugly-looking guy at the next table who is trying to hear what we're talking about."

"Better come to my office," suggested Hunt.

In Hunt's office—which had once been a *pension* for English tourists—Hambledon brought him up-to-date with news of Armand de Rollencourt and Christopher Hardy, with whom they had shared that adventure on the roads. He also described life in the farmhouse at Grancourt with Madeleine Delaroche, and Armand's mother and sister, and the two Germans who were billeted on them.

Chas Hunt seemed to be amused.

"I guess you're pretty deep in love with one of those women, and I guess that the girl you love is a hundred-per-cent. pro de Gaulle and is dragging you into the net. Am I wrong?"

"Dead wrong," answered Hambledon, with conscienceless insincerity.

"Liar!" answered Hunt. "I can see the truth in your eyes, buddy—that soft look of romantic love."

Edward waved all this away.

"Cut it out," he said. "I've come here to talk reasonably, and to ask you to lend a hand in a good work."

"Tell me the worst," said Hunt. "How many bucks?"

"Not a nickel," answered Edward. "I've come here to get a few papers which will help the escape of British soldiers still in France and young Frenchmen in hiding from the Gestapo."

"What sort of papers?" asked Hunt cautiously.

"*Cartes d'identité* with the Vichy stamp. I will provide the photos. *Sauf-conduits*, also stamped by the Vichy police. The signatures of Laval and Pétain. Exit permits to Spain with authority to proceed on business affairs."

Chas Hunt laughed loudly.

"How in hell do you think you're going to get them?"

"It's easy," said Edward. "It's all arranged. There's a very friendly guy in a subordinate position here. He sits in an outer room of Pétain's headquarters. He used to be a French newspaper man and one of your pals."

Chas Hunt stubbed out the end of a Camel cigarette.

"How do you know?" he asked. "What's his name?"

Edward lowered his voice and gave the name, at which Hunt raised his eyebrows with astonishment.

"What, that fellow? He used to dine with me at Fouquet's now and then."

Edward nodded.

"All I ask you to do is to go and see him and say that your American friend has arrived from Grancourt Notre-Dame and would much like to have lunch with him tomorrow at your private apartment. If you could arrange that little lunch, Chas, I'll stand you an excellent dinner in Paris as soon as this war is over. And it will be over all the sooner if you can do this favour for me."

"Now, look here," said Hunt.

He was just a bit scared about that lunch in his private rooms. He didn't want to get mixed up in any dirty work, well, any work which could be held against him by French police or German agents. He was not reassured by Edward's easy-going assertion that there was nothing to it. No possible suspicion could be aroused by an American newspaper man entertaining an official attached to Marshal Pétain. But Hunt was touched when Edward reminded him of many poor devils who were waiting for a chance of escape which might be denied them if Hunt refused this little service.

"Well, that's O.K. with me," he said at last. "I'll do it, but against my better judgment. And if you'll take a bit of advice from me, buddy, you'll go back pretty damn quick to your mother in Massachusetts. You're just asking for trouble, and the kind of trouble that leads to a white wall and a firing-squad."

"Nothing like that, I hope," said Edward.

The luncheon party in Hunt's rooms was entirely without drama of any obvious or alarming kind, though Hunt was nervous, and at the back of his mind Hambledon was amused by a sense of playing a part behind the scenes of French history. A very small part in a very great drama.

The French official, who had been a newspaper man in Paris—the editor of a political review of high standing—was suave and conversational. He discussed French literature, the charm of Vichy before the war, and the difficulty of understanding American politics, and especially the methods of electing a president.

Before leaving, he turned to Hambledon with a question:

"Do I understand that you are going to Paris?"

"I have an idea of doing so," answered Edward.

"In that case, may I entrust you with some family papers which have a slight importance?"

"Certainly," answered Edward, "with pleasure."

"They're addressed to a cousin of mine who would be most glad to meet you. In the Avenue Victor Hugo. He is a most intelligent fellow, but nothing would budge him from Paris, not even the Germans."

He handed Edward a big envelope filled with papers.

"You will take care of them?"

"You can rely on that."

"A thousand thanks. It has been a great pleasure to meet you."

He departed with a charming smile.

"Gosh!" exclaimed Chas Hunt, striding about the room and looking ruffled. "All this is very dangerous."

"I guess he delivered the goods," answered Edward. "That's the value of having a friend at Court."

"If those papers are found on you," said Hunt warningly, "not even your American citizenship will get you out of the hoosegow."

"It'll be bad luck if anybody searches me on the way to Paris," said Edward, light-heartedly. "Well, thanks a lot, Hunt."

"Ned Hambledon," said Hunt, putting his hand on Edward's shoulder, "you're a brave man, but this isn't your line of business. Get back to Massachusetts, laddy. The Gestapo have nasty forms of torture."

"Oh, I'm going back one day," answered Edward. "See you in New York, some time."

XXV

PARIS AGAIN.

Edward Hambledon paced down its familiar streets with a sense of tragedy strong within him. He felt very lonely, though many people had returned and the city was not so deserted as when he had left it. But all his friends, or nearly all, had gone, and in their place German officers and men were in possession. He saw a German guard, headed by a military band, marching towards the Arc de Triomphe. German officers were sitting outside Fouquet's, up the Avenue des Champs-Élysées, though it was autumn weather now. They passed through the swing-doors of the Café de la Paix. They stared into the shop windows along the Boulevard des Italiens and the Rue Royale and the Avenue de l'Opéra. There was a coming and going of military cars outside the Hôtel Crillon. The Parisians passed them as though they did not exist, never glancing at them. Only in the lowest haunts of Montmartre was there any association between German soldiers and French women. Edward did not penetrate into those quarters, but in the Rue Montmartre, up which he walked to the Père Jean one evening, he saw little French sluts in the embrace of German soldiers, some of whom were drunk. Not a pleasant sight. Hambledon turned his head away from them and felt sick.

He went into the Père Jean, where he found the *patron* and his wife and the girl Suzanne, and the old Englishman, Robinson, who had come in as usual for his coffee and game of Patience. It seemed a year since he had seen them and he was touched by their greeting as though he were their long-lost son.

"*Monsieur Edouard!*" cried Madame Marchand. "*Quel plaisir de vous revoir!*"

The *patron* held his hand in an iron grip, and Suzanne gave a cry of astonishment at the sight of him. A few mechanics and taxi-drivers were having their evening meal and there were two *midinettes* and a solitary well-dressed girl reading a novel at one of the small tables.

"How goes it in Paris?" asked Edward presently.

Madame Marchand raised her hands.

"We exist. That is all!"

"And the Germans? How are they behaving?"

It was the *patron* who answered.

"On the whole, they are correct. On the whole, they behave well. There are, of course, drunken orgies in dirty places. But certainly, as a rule, they are correct. One must say that."

Suzanne gave a shrill and bitter laugh.

"I wish to be sick when I hear that word 'correct.' They have destroyed France, but they are 'correct.' They rob the pictures out of the Louvre, but they are 'correct.' They seize all the food in France and if one German is killed in a back street they shoot ten Frenchmen, but they are 'correct.' "

"The authorities are ruthless," admitted the *patron;* "but the rank and file and the officers conduct themselves reasonably well. They pay for what they buy. That is something. They are polite, which is also something."

Suzanne laughed again harshly and with a shrill voice.

"It is the German character. They killed my man, but they would like me to love them. They do not understand because I am as cold as ice and do not look at them. They have the instinct of bandits and assassins. After their dirty work they wish to amuse themselves and be happy with their victims."

Some of the people in the restaurant joined in this argument. Old Robinson, looking up from his Patience cards, made an observation of a dark nature.

"The Germans want to be loved. They smash their way through Europe in a spirit of loving-kindness."

One of the *midinettes* had something to say.

"I serve, as you know, outside the Magazins du Louvre. German soldiers speak to me in bad French. They are annoyed when I refuse to smile at their clumsy and disgusting flirtations. Other girls are not unfriendly. They have no loyalty. They have no decency. They ought to have all their clothes torn off and their hair cut off."

One of the mechanics laughed harshly.

"That is what will happen to them one day. When General de Gaulle comes back with an Army of Liberation."

"When will that be, my friend?" asked another of the mechanics. "In ten years or in twenty? The Germans have us under their heels. They are masters of Europe. For my part, I think old Pétain is right. A little collaboration is necessary. The Germans are not all bad. Some of them are almost human. We have to make the best of a bad business."

Suzanne answered him fiercely:

"That is to say, you will lick your chains. Play the dirty coward."

"I have only one life," said the mechanic, "and I believe in the brotherhood of man."

Suzanne gave her shrill laugh again.

"Then you'll believe anything!"

The argument continued and boiled up hotly and then subsided when two German soldiers came in. They were non-commissioned officers and saluted the company before sitting at a small table and staring at the menu. They looked uncomfortable in the dead silence of this restaurant. Suzanne ignored them until Madame Marchand whispered to her. Then she went to the table with tight lips and a pallid face and misery in her eyes.

One of the Germans spoke a little French.

"*S'il vous plait, mademoiselle.*"

He ordered a plate of tripe, and smiled at Suzanne in a friendly way, but the smile faded from his lips because of her white hostile face and the hatred in her eyes.

Edward went to his studio. There was a new concierge, who did not know him but let him in when he showed his keys and explained his previous occupation.

His rooms smelt damp. His books and canvases were filmed with dust. The window curtains were drawn as he had left them at dawn when he went away with Kit Hardy.

Three or four letters lay on the mat inside his door. They bore American stamps. Letters from home. They must have been delivered after the German entry of Paris.

The concierge had come upstairs with him as though not quite certain that he was the rightful occupant of these rooms.

"Are you staying here?" he asked.

"Only a night or two."

"The German police will want your *carte d'identité* and other papers. We have to report every inhabitant. They keep a sharp eye on everyone."

"Without doubt," answered Edward.

The concierge went downstairs again and Edward opened his letters and read them.

His people were worried about him.

My dear Edward (wrote his father), *your mother and I are expecting you back any day now. We hope very much that you will get out of France without difficulty or danger. The situation there seems desperate as I write. The French dêbâcle is mysterious and lamentable and everybody here fears that England cannot stand up alone against an all-powerful Germany. This is a distressing thought and I confess that it keeps me awake at night. England's downfall would be a great disaster to civilization. All the same, I earnestly hope that we shall not be dragged into this war by Mr. Roosevelt, whose foreign policy and latest utterances are highly dangerous and likely to involve us in this European conflict from which we should keep well away. My friends of the Tavern Club are mainly of this opinion, and their dislike of Mr. Roosevelt is deepening into something like passionate hostility. . . . Penny is having a good time and has done a lot of riding this summer. We do not see eye to eye on world affairs or domestic politics. She is fanatical in her adoration of Mr. Roosevelt and thinks we ought to jump into this war at England's side. We argue but don't quarrel, she being a very good comrade of mine, bless her pretty face. She goes to too many cocktail parties with her beau Spike Brandon who, in my opinion, which I keep secret, is not worthy to tie up her shoelaces.*

There was a postscript.

We are really anxious about you. If you need any money send me a cable.

Hambledon read through the other letters. His sister Penny was also worried.

For goodness' sake come back, Edward. Don't get caught by the Blond Beast. Don't stay in Paris when the German Luftwaffe is overhead. Take care of yourself and get out of France while the going is good. . . . I have been having a lovely summer. . . .

There was a narrative of swimming, boating, riding, and a round of parties.

His brother Tiny scrawled a line.

Why in hell don't you come back before you get caught in the furnace fires? One doesn't walk between two express trains heading for a collision. If Roosevelt drags us into this war, and he's heading that way, I shall become a passive resister for conscience' sake, and also to save my skin, which at the moment is very bronzed after sunbathing and swimming. I don't want to die fighting England's wars. No, sir! I cherish my young life and all the things that differentiate intelligent man from his gorilla ancestry. I hope to get my last play put on as a try-out in Chicago. It's good. It's a flaming indictment of war, but not without humour and an irony which will be above the heads of those dumb-bells who like the leg shows in Broadway. However, I'll tell you all about that when you arrive. Don't linger as an onlooker of hell's kitchen. We're getting a bit scared about you, knowing your romantic tendencies.

Hambledon read these letters with a smile about his lips, which faded out when he dropped them to the floor and went into a brown study in that studio which for him was haunted with ghosts of a world which had gone. Olga. Many pretty girls. French and American friends. Odette, the daughter of the concierge. The ghost of himself new to Paris, mad keen on his painting, curious about life, ardent in his first love, a gay fellow laughing a lot, singing in his bath, shouting to Odette while she was dusting in the next room.

Those letters from home were a reminder of another way of life—the American way of life which was pretty good. Swimming, boating, riding by the lake of Assawampsett. What could be better? Over there was peace and plenty. Over there, as though in another planet, there was no menace of war, no realization of war. Penny went to her cocktail parties and had a good time. Of course, they were interested in this European war, but only as flaring headlines and dramatic news which made the papers interesting, but instantly forgotten when local politics or the daily excitements of domestic life thrust them away for more personal interest. It would be the sensible thing to go back, even though he would go back to a purposeless life. More reasonable to go back. Should he go back and quit this drama in France after seeing the first act? Why in hell did he want to stay and let himself get entangled in this underground stuff which wasn't without risk? Why did he know perfectly well inside himself that he would go back to an old farmhouse near Tours?

What was drawing him back? To help in the escape of French prisoners of war who wished to fight for de Gaulle? Yes. That wasn't a bad motive. The idea interested him and there was a touch of drama in it, a bit of risk which he was ready to take for a good cause. He was all for de Gaulle. But that was not the chief pull back. If he were dead honest with himself—and he wanted to be dead honest—it was Lucile who pulled him back and kept him from any boat which might be sailing for New York. She had taken the place of Olga, though in a different way. He loved the look of her—her little dark head, the grace of her body, her play of expression, the gestures of her fine delicate hands—beautifully modelled they were—and her sensitive mouth. But it was her spirit which put a spell on him, her intelligence, her character. She had courage beyond that of most women. She was ready to face death for the sake of France. She had been charming to him. They had spoken no word of love, but he loved her, not with passion as he had loved Olga, but with respect and devotion. It was she, Lucile de Rollencourt, who called him back into the danger zone where as an American he had no business, strictly speaking, as an outsider.

He met certain people in Paris. The cousin of the Vichy official, a former school friend of Lucile's, who was the daughter of a French General; a French naval man on the retired list; a publisher of prints and etchings; a former member of the staff on the *Echo de Paris*.

They seemed to be pretty far forward in organizing an underground movement of resistance and had made a chain of friends across France to help the escape of young Frenchmen eager to fight for de Gaulle. They were all expecting a visit from Edward Hambledon by some secret message which had reached them.

"We shall be ready in a few days to send some of our men to Grancourt Notre-Dame," said Marguerite Germain, who had been to school with Lucile.

"They are now in hiding with our friends at various stages of the route. The Bois des Fées is the last link of our chain in Occupied France. Give my dearest love to Lucile, who stands at this critical post."

She was in her apartment in the Avenue Foch. It was elegantly furnished and there were some good modern pictures on the walls. She was dressed in a simple black frock, cut low at the neck.

"This is only the beginning of French resistance," she said. "One day it will spread throughout France and gather strength. We have many devoted friends already willing to take every risk."

She held out her hand to Hambledon.

"You are one of us," she told him. "We are deeply grateful for your help."

Hambledon took his leave. That last phrase—"You are one of us"—remained in his mind. Yes, if he went back to Grancourt Notre-Dame he would be in this business—up to the neck.

He went back to Grancourt Notre-Dame.

PART II

AMERICA

I

Anthony Hambledon, brother of Edward, who had lost himself somewhere in France, stood on the wooden platform of an old windmill in Lakeside, Massachusetts, and gazed at the beauty of the world about him and did not seem to like it. He groaned heavily like a man in anguish and uttered the words "Oh, God!" as though praying for relief from life.

He stood six-foot-three in his bare feet, and was a fine figure of a young man upon whom the sun of Massachusetts shone warmly in that early morning of a September day. He stood there almost naked, having just sprung out of bed where he had spent a restless night, flung off his pyjamas, and put on a pair of white linen shorts. His body was richly tanned at the end of a hot summer. His face and neck were deeply coloured, as brown as those of a Red Indian—one of those Redskins who in former days had possessed this land with its lakes and woods, a great solitude in which they were lonely.

Anthony Hambledon, called Tiny by his family and friends, had taken possession of this old windmill, long disused, as his own sanctuary and hide-away. Not even his sister Penny, who dared most things, ventured to come in here without first giving a Coo-ee! and asking permission to enter. Otherwise there was a row about it. Here in a circular room he had his books, writing-table, and bed, with a small cooking stove upon which he could make a meal at any time of the day or night. In winter he could keep himself warm by another stove fed by wood which he could get near at hand from the dead branches of silver birches. In this study, as he called it, he could escape from family discussions, week-end guests in his father's house a quarter of a mile away, and be entirely alone with himself and his thoughts.

Here he had written his one successful play and sixteen unsuccessful plays, mostly unproduced. Here lately—that is to say for six months or more—he had worried himself by secret brooding and disturbed nights because of increasing passion for a certain lady who happened to be the wife of another man and very loyal to her marriage vows, though kind, friendly, and humorous to Anthony Hambledon who, as very well she knew, adored her body and mind. That was Cynthia Birch from London, England, a refugee from the German Blitz because of her small daughter aged four.

Tiny Hambledon had been thinking of her during the night when he ought to have been sleeping. She had disturbed his mind a lot by telling him that she had made up her mind to go back to England. She had laughed with her usual humour when he had asked what in hell he was going to do without her for intelligent conversation, sympathetic aid, and understanding friendship.

"You don't need me as much as all that," she told him. "You won't miss me after the first week. I'm only one of your bad habits, like cigarette smoking. You like to argue with me, and try how far you can go in anti-British prejudice before you get me angry. I must say it has been very good to see so much of you, but I've wasted your time, Tiny, and created scandal in your family. Anyhow, I must get back to England. I can't stand this exile any longer."

That is what she had told him when he was alone with her last night. He had argued with her and pleaded with her, and walked up and down her room like a tiger, and then he tried to kiss her after telling her that he loved her like hell. That had been a mistake. She had pushed him away with both hands and her face had become very white for a moment, and she had told him to go. He had gone and slammed the door behind him. No wonder he hadn't slept very well.

Standing there on his wooden platform like a figure in bronze, he stared at the loveliness of the world about him with a heavy frown which made a tuck in his forehead. Below him, a few hundred yards away, were the paddocks with their white rails, and the jumps which Penny took when she did her morning rides. Beyond them was the golf-course which his father had laid out at great expense before the depression of '29 which had curtailed his income. Beyond was the lake of Assawampsett, like molten metal under the morning sun, already beginning to burn. It had burnt the golf-course brown, except on the greens which were kept watered. Woods, mostly of silver birch, stretched as far as the eye could see beyond the lake, with a clearing here and there showing the fields with thin soil through which bare gleaming rocks cropped up, as all over this State of Massachusetts. There had been times when Tiny Hambledon had thought all this beautiful. Even as a small boy, released from school in Boston for long stretches here, he had thought this place a paradise. He had had grand times here, swimming, boating, riding, sitting on the old rocks, reading about Red Indians, playing Red Indian games in the woods. Now this morning it all seemed hateful because of that scene last night with Cynthia.

A Coo-ee! came up to him. Penny came riding through the paddocks, taking one of the jumps on her young mare with the white socks. She wore a yellow polo shirt and a pair of white shorts. Her arms and legs were as brown as his, and her blue eyes were set in a tanned face below her mop of straw-coloured hair.

She sang out to him:

"'Morning, Tiny! Come over to breakfast. There's a letter from Edward—the first since five months. Anyhow, he's still alive, but very mysterious. Mother is crazy at having heard from him at last."

Tiny Hambledon answered her from his wooden platform.

"He's probably caught by some demoiselle if I know anything about our kid brother. I'll be along soon."

"And, Tiny," called out Penelope Hambledon, from the back of her brown mare, "I want you to come to lunch today for a special reason."

"What's that?" asked her brother, suspiciously.

She laughed before answering.

"We have a very nice guest. A young English naval officer from the battleship *Rodney*. I met him in Boston."

"Oh, hell!" said Tiny.

"He's very charming. Terribly good looking. You'll like him."

"I'm darned sure I won't," answered this very tall young man, who looked down upon his sister from the high platform of his windmill. "I don't like English affectation, and I don't want to be patronized as though I belonged to an inferior race. I've had that before. It gets my goat."

"Dick Arkwright isn't like that!" cried Penelope. "He thinks we're all wonderful. He's crazy about Boston and American food and the American way of life. . . . So come to lunch, Tiny, there's a dear."

Her brown mare with the white socks was getting restless and danced sideways.

"Steady, Bess. Steady, old girl!"

She waved a hand, turned her mare, and shot off across the brown grass towards the parental house, visible beyond the golf-course, with its slate roof and brown walls based upon primeval rock, cropping up from the soil and making its foundations.

Before putting on a blue shirt and going over to breakfast with the family, Tiny Hambledon strode into his circular room, dialled a number on his telephone, heard a woman's voice answer, and said: "That you, Cynthia?"

"Who else could it be?" she asked with a laugh. "How do you feel this morning, Tiny?"

"A wreck," he told her. "I didn't get a wink last night. I lay cursing myself and suffering the tortures of a damned soul."

She laughed again, and he liked to hear that English laugh.

"Indigestion?" she asked. "Pork pies or something?"

"Conscience, lady," he answered. "I behaved like a primitive man. I want to lie down at your feet. I want to grovel. Anyhow, I want you to forgive me."

"Oh, there's nothing to forgive!" she told him. "I've been so glad of your friendship. Don't let's spoil it—especially now when I'm going away pretty soon."

Anthony Hambledon groaned slightly before he answered.

"Say, you make me want to burst into tears. The thought of your going away just makes me suicidal. I've been in seventh heaven every time I've come to see you."

"Come again!" she answered with that little low laugh. "Come this evening, Tiny. Read me out the last act of your new play."

"Do you mean it?" he asked anxiously. "Have you really forgiven me for trying to kiss you last night? And then my rage when you wouldn't?"

"All is forgiven!" she told him lightly. "As long as you don't do it again. Nine o'clock?"

"Nine o'clock though the heavens fall," he answered. He wanted to say other things, but she had put up the receiver after saying: "That's good."

He felt better after that telephone conversation. He felt strong enough in spirit to shave himself. The dark misery of wakeful hours in the night had passed. Anyhow, he wanted breakfast. Even hopeless lovers are hungry in the morning.

II

THE ARRIVAL IN Massachusetts of Cynthia Birch and her little daughter Tessa was pleasant and emotional for those who first met her, and were anxious, in the American way, to offer her all kinds of kindness and hospitality.

The Blitz over England in 1940 had horrified them, and the heroism of the English people in standing up to it—"London can take it!"—"Coventry can take it!"—stirred their admiration in a very profound way. The ladies of Boston and other American cities organized "Aid For Britain" and "Bundles for Britain" and gave their time as well as their money—heaps of it—in providing clothes and comforts and medical supplies for those who had lost their homes, and were victims of this atrocious form of war.

The mothers of Britain were invited to bring their children to the United States, and the only restrictions to this wide-open offer were the guarantee of financial sponsors required by the American Government, and the sinking of ships by German U-boats—terrifying in their toll of life.

Mrs. Hambledon had been one of those who gave her guarantee that an English mother and child should not become a burden to the United States, although the British Government was niggardly in its permission for English money to be brought out and exchanged for American dollars. Well-to-do people in England who parted from their children could not provide for them, and had to rely upon the generosity of Americans who were willing to receive them.

Mrs. Hambledon was delighted to receive Cynthia Birch and her little daughter—in spite of some opposition from members of her family. A letter had come from Cynthia's father, Mr. Henry Ottershaw, with whom they had made friends on a Mediterranean cruise. He had explained the need of a guarantee, and the urgent anxiety of himself and his son-in-law regarding Cynthia and her child.

"Send a cable at once," said Mrs. Hambledon, in her brisk, masterful way.

"Of course we shall be terribly glad to guarantee the poor dears. I wish we could guarantee all the mothers and children of England."

Mr. Edward Hambledon, senior, looked up from his *New York Times* and smiled at his wife across the breakfast-table.

"I'd hate to cramp your enthusiasm," he said, "but is it quite wise? This English girl and her baby might be rather a tie on us, don't you think? And I'm not sure that I can afford to add to my household expenses, with income-tax mounting, and the high cost of living getting higher every month—mainly because of Mr. Roosevelt and his lavish hand with public money, and his pandering to revolutionary Labour."

"You're talking nonsense, Edward," answered Mrs. Hambledon. "My heart bleeds for those bombed-out people in England. If I had to go without bread and butter I wouldn't refuse shelter to any of them."

"Bravo, Mother!" cried Penelope, who had just drunk her morning glass of orange juice. "We ought to have been in this war long ago.

The English people are fighting our war and saving our skins. The least we can do is to open a way of escape for some of their women and children."

That tall fellow, Tiny, who happened to have come in to breakfast from his mill house, grinned at his sister and ranged himself by the side of his father.

"That kind of talk makes me tired, Penny, my child. England wants us to pull her chestnuts out of the fire again. English propaganda is trying its best to lure us into another world war, in which personally I'm not interested. As for having that English girl here, I think it would be a great mistake. You know what they are like—all affectation and snootiness. Take it from me, she would spoil the charm of this simple home life, and once here we couldn't get rid of the lass. We should have her on our hands year after year. Frightful prospect."

"You're without a soul and without a conscience," answered Penny. "Pass me that mess of pottage, buddy."

Mrs. Hambledon had her own way. She always had her own way, being a lady of character, with courage enough to revolt against the Back Bay traditions of Boston which belonged to a ruling and reactionary caste. The guarantee was cabled to England. An old frame cottage at the end of the estate on the shore of Lake Assawampsett was swept and garnished for the arrival of the young English mother and her little girl. Jake, the hired man, colour-washed the ceilings and repaired the boiler. Mrs. Hambledon bought new chintz coverings for the chairs in Boston. She carried over from her own house several nice etchings and collected editions of poems by Tennyson, Wordsworth, and Shelley with the latest copy of *Vogue* and some old numbers of *Harper's Magazine*. For the little girl she provided some dolls and comic animals—bought at great expense—from Schwarz in Boston.

Mrs. Hambledon's eldest and long-legged son was coerced to go with Penny to meet the refugees on their arrival at La Guardia airfield outside New York. His plea that he was engaged on the last scene of an epoch-making play left his mother cold.

"That will wait," she said firmly. "It's less important than meeting Cynthia Birch, and I can't go myself as I'm presiding at the General Committee of Bundles for Britain."

"Hell!" said Tiny under his breath, but he accepted the inevitable, and drove his Packard at a furious rate to New York, secretly amused because even Penny, who was very fearless, looked a bit scared now and then and warned him about traffic cops.

The Clipper arrived out of the blue at the appointed tick of time. From it descended several film stars, whose faces were familiar to Penny, half a dozen elderly men who might have been British diplomats, two newspaper correspondents, various foreigners of unguessable nationality, who had doubtless escaped from the clutches of the Gestapo in the occupied countries of Europe, and a number of young mothers with their children—refugees from the Blitz over Britain—by way of Lisbon.

Among them were Cynthia Birch and little Tessa.

Penny spotted her first.

"I believe that's Cynthia. How English looking and how adorable!"

"Think so?" asked Tiny, staring grumpily at the girl pointed out by his sister. "That wild-eyed wench with the flat chest and the long legs? She hasn't combed her hair lately, maybe."

So he spoke, but to himself he thought other things. He thought this girl with tousled fair hair and blue eyes rather far apart—tall and slim and long-legged, in a shabby blue frock which left her brown arms bare to the shoulders—looked like a wood nymph who had come to New York from some English forest. There was an untamed look in her eyes, he thought. A wood nymph would have eyes like that, a little wild and a little wondering. She had a thin face revealing her cheek-bones, and a pointed chin and a mouth without lipstick. A little girl clutched her hand, while in her other arm she carried a golliwog and a teddy bear.

Penny was the first to greet Cynthia with effusive affection and real emotion.

"How wonderful that you've come! I do hope you're going to be happy in the United States after all you've been through. I'm Penelope Hambledon. They call me Penny. This is my big brother Anthony. We call him Tiny. And this is little Tessa! How terribly sweet she is! Did she like the trip in the Clipper?"

"Not much," answered Cynthia. "She was sick a good deal."

"Yes, I was sick over everybody," said Tessa, as though proud of this achievement.

When Cynthia gave her hand to Tiny she looked up into his eyes in a frank, unshy way.

"You're a long way up!" she said, with a slight smile.

"Yes, I have to stoop to my friends," he told her.

On the way through New York—where they had tea at the Plaza—she was rather silent, and Penny did most of the chattering. But she made one or two remarks which interested Tiny.

"I feel that I have come to another planet."

"It's a friendly part of the planet," said Penelope reassuringly. "Everyone will try to make you happy here. And you'll love Boston and the country round about. It's very English, I believe."

"Do you ever think about the war in Europe?" asked Cynthia. "It must be difficult for your minds to reach as far as that. I mean, all these people here in the New York streets. It can't mean very much to them, except as newspaper headlines."

"That girl has a lot of sense in her head," thought Tiny, over his steering-wheel. "She talks straight. She doesn't gush like most English girls I've met."

He could see her face reflected in the mirror on his car, and when they were held up by traffic blocks he saw her gazing up at the skyscrapers, towering high above them.

Once he spoke to her over his shoulder.

"What do you think of little old New York? Not much like London?"

He heard her laugh before answering.

"Not a bit like London! Wonderful—and frightening."

"Frightening? Do you mean it scares you?"

"It might be a city in Mars," she answered. "It doesn't belong to our old-fashioned civilization."

"It sure doesn't!" he agreed.

She made one other remark about New York several blocks farther on.

"It's a good thing you're outside Hitler's bombing range. Those skyscrapers would make quite a mess if they were hit."

"Lady," said Tiny Hambledon, "that's one of the good reasons why the United States should keep neutral in this war, in spite of Mr. Roosevelt's bias towards plunging us all into hell fire. I don't mind telling you that I'm a hundred-per-cent. Isolationist. I hope that doesn't shock your English sensibilities?"

He saw her smile as he looked into the mirror, and their eyes met in the reflection of that bit of glass.

"You'll have to come in one day," she answered. "You won't be able to keep out."

Penny greeted this remark with enthusiasm.

"That's my own conviction. Tiny and I have the most terrible arguments about it. He poses as a pacifist."

"Sure, I'm a man of peace," said Tiny. "If I were a Christian I should quote the words of Christ."

Further conversation on this subject was interrupted by little Tessa.

"When are we going to have tea, Mummy? I'm getting hungry, and so is Golliwog."

They had tea at the Plaza, where Tiny made friends with Tessa by creating a very good rabbit out of a table napkin, and otherwise entertaining her while Penny was putting Cynthia Birch wise to the social set-up in Lakeside, where the cottage awaited her.

"It all sounds very pleasant," said Cynthia. "It's all very kind of everybody."

"This girl," thought Tiny, "keeps her dignity, although she's a refugee who's going to live on the charity of my family. She doesn't wallow in gratitude. Thank God she doesn't gush. She's one of Shakespeare's young women. She might have stepped out of the woodland scenes in *As You Like It!* She's not unattractive."

His first impressions of Cynthia Birch were fairly favourable.

III

THE SOCIAL SET in this corner of Massachusetts gave the friendliest welcome to young Mrs. Birch and her child among other refugees from England to whom they had guaranteed shelter and support. The Hambledon family and their friends heaped kindness upon her, and invited her to their charming homes scattered around the lake of Assawampsett, to which Taunton was the nearest town, with Boston forty miles away. They invited her to luncheon parties, tea parties—it was in compliment to the English national habit that they provided orange pekoe tea—cocktail parties, and dinner parties. Mrs. Hawley Hunt, mother of Chas Hunt, a newspaper man now in Vichy, was a devotee of music and came several times to Cynthia's cottage to carry her off to Boston for a symphony concert. She was a little hurt when Cynthia made excuses for not going, because of Tessa, whom she could not leave alone.

"Oh, that's easy!" cried Mrs. Hawley Hunt, who was the kindest-hearted lady. "I will send round Paula, my Portuguese maid. She's very good with children."

But there were many times, not only with Mrs. Hawley Hunt, but with Penny Hambledon and others, when Cynthia had to excuse herself from social engagements because Tessa had sprung a temperature—the sharp fluctuations of the Massachusetts climate were hard on English children—or because Tessa had a slight chill, or a touch of acidosis, and in any case wept bitterly if left too long with strangers, however kind, without her mummy. It was disappointing to the Wakefields of Taunton, who had invited a party of young people to meet her. It was disappointing to the Zimmermanns, who had a summer country house not far from that of the Hambledons. They had asked her repeatedly to play croquet with a bunch of boys and girls from Boston who came down for week-ends. At the fourth time of asking, Mrs. Zimmermann showed some slight resentment.

"That child can't always be sick!" she remarked, when a little note came from Cynthia. "Maybe young Mrs. Birch doesn't like our American ways."

"That sure may be so," answered Mr. Zimmermann. "She struck me as being a very haughty young woman, and as cold as ice, like so many English. Well, it won't hurt us. I ain't worrying, Momma."

She was the subject of frequent conversation at the Hambledons. Penny fell in love with her straight away and never let a morning pass, unless she were in Boston or New York, without riding round to Maple Cottage with some little gift of fruit or flowers or a box of candies for Tessa. Dismounting from her brown mare with the white socks, she would utter a Red Indian cry, and call out in a high-pitched voice:

"'Morning, Cynthia! How's Tessa? How's life?"

Cynthia's head would appear out of the bedroom window.

"Hullo, Penny! Sorry I can't come down. I'm just giving Tessa her bath."

She always had a gipsy look, with bare legs and feet in sandals and shabby frocks which no American girl would have worn; or she would appear from behind the house where she had been hanging out Tessa's frocks to dry after washing them in the kitchen.

"Come in for a few minutes. Do you mind if I turn on the wireless? I haven't heard the morning news."

Penny noticed that she was hungry for the day's news and clung to the radio. Often when she came round to the Hambledons for an hour in the evening after putting Tessa to bed, the radio was switched on, but it seemed to stimulate general conversation, and everybody started talking, except Cynthia. Tiny, who liked watching her face, saw how she was listening intently to news from Europe, ignoring the talk which swirled around her. Once when news was rather worse than usual—the British were having a bad time in North Africa and had been beaten back into Egypt—he saw that her eyes became wet for a moment until she blinked away her tears.

"That girl takes the war hard," thought Tiny. "And her heart's over there in Europe. She finds this an exile, and I guess that all this chatter is very trying to her. We're not interested in her war, as she said, except as exciting stuff for newspaper headlines."

His father was very courteous to her in his old-fashioned way, and rather liked her at first.

"An intelligent young woman," he remarked once or twice. "Not that I agree with her point of view, of course. But I don't blame her for it. I'll say it's natural!"

He had drawn her out one evening when several friends had come in to meet her.

"I suppose England can take care of this war, Mrs. Birch?" he said, during a pause in the general conversation.

She looked at him in her frank, wide-eyed way, as though she did not understand.

"Take care of it?"

"I mean England will be able to build up her strength in man-power and win the last battles as she always does?"

His friends—they were the Wakefields and the Hunts—listened for her answer. They seemed interested.

Cynthia was slow in answering—she was thinking it out, and perhaps wondering how frank she ought to be among these Americans.

"I don't think we can beat the Germans," she said, "with our own man-power. We haven't much of a population, even including the Dominions. You see, the Navy and Air Force take a lot of our men. Then we have to keep the factories going. We can't raise a big army on the Continental scale."

Mr. John J. Wakefield, a big man with a big, clean-shaven face, took a cigar from his mouth and answered her good-humouredly.

"That's a frank answer, Mrs. Birch, and I guess it's true."

Mr. Robert Hawley Hunt, the well-known lawyer in Boston, had a few remarks to make. Because of the great heat on this September evening he had taken off his jacket, and was sitting in a white silk shirt and a pair of linen trousers.

"Some of your British propagandists over here are hinting that Great Britain can only win the war with the aid of American man-power. Not that they say it straight out, but reading between the lines, or behind their masks, that's what they mean. Now it would be a good thing for the English people to know the dead-line limit in the American mind."

Mr. Hambledon looked over to his friend and gave a laugh.

"Do you happen to know it, Bob? That's more than most of us do. Some pretty confused thinking goes on in these United States. We're hopelessly divided about almost everything."

Mr. Robert Hawley Hunt seemed sure of his fround.

"Now, I'm telling you. Take any American mind you like. Take any American mother, and I'll bet you'll find one conviction, and that's unshakable."

"I'll be glad to know," answered Mr. Hambledon, with humorous scepticism.

"I'm telling you, Ted. It's just this: We're willing to give all aid to Britain, for whom we have a great admiration because of her courageous resistance to Nazi might. Yes, sir! as far as supplying her with the munitions of war. We'd be sorry to see England go down, because of her great contributions to civilization, including Shakespeare and all that. But there's not an American father or mother in this country, as far as I know them, and I know them pretty well, who will allow their boys to be sent overseas this time to fight in that hell's brew called Europe. All aid to Britain, but no Expeditionary Force. And if you'll like to take the opinion of this small group I'll be glad. Mrs. Hambledon, I put it to you."

Mrs. Hambledon, who was president and chairwoman of many committees for "Aid to Britain" and "Bundles for Britain," became thoughtful. She was a good-looking lady, with fair hair turning a little grey. She had a look of vitality and efficiency, fully borne out by her social and political activities. She answered after a slight hesitation.

"I bleed at the heart for dear old England and all the suffering which she has to endure in this frightful war. I feel I want to give all my money and all my work to relieve the sufferings of their heroic people. But I don't want our boys to die on European battlefields as so many of their fathers did—in vain."

Mr. Robert Hawley Hunt smiled and nodded.

"You've said it, Mrs. Hambledon. And now you, Mrs. Wakefield."

Mrs. Wakefield was very strongly against American youth being sacrificed in Europe. She had no patience with Mr. Roosevelt, who, in the most crafty and unconstitutional way, was trying to get the American people involved in the struggle. Step by step he was luring them on to that doom. Of course she loved England, and could almost scream when she read of the bombing of civilians. She had stayed several times in London at Brown's Hotel.

"And what about you, Tiny, my boy?" asked Mr. Robert Hawley Hunt. "As one of the young men who would be asked to fight, how do you feel about it?"

Tiny Hambledon, sitting in a low chair with his long legs outstretched, gave an uneasy laugh.

"Oh, leave me out of it! I'm against war, anyhow. I don't think this war ought to have happened."

Mr. Hunt turned to Cynthia with a smile.

"You see, Mrs. Birch, this is a cross-section of American opinion. So you mustn't look for millions of American boys to weigh down the scales in man-power. We learnt a few things last time. We helped to win the war but we got no gratitude. We were called Uncle Shylock when we asked for payment of war debts."

"Leave that out, Bob," said Mr. Hambledon. "It's another subject, and some of us think we were in the wrong in demanding payment which could only be made in goods we refused to receive and wouldn't allow to come in."

He turned to Cynthia with his friendly smile.

"What have you to say to all this?" he asked. "Whatever you say won't give any offence. This is Liberty Hall. We believe in free speech."

Cynthia saw the eyes of these friendly people watching her. She saw that long-limbed young man called Tiny looking at her curiously. She often found his eyes regarding her as though she were a strange kind of animal and rather amusing to him.

"I don't see any logic in your point of view," she answered, in her clear English voice.

She noticed that Penny had just come in. She was wearing an evening frock as though she had been to a dance or was going to one. That answer Cynthia had made seemed to cause a moment's silence. It was broken by Mr. Robert Hunt.

"Say, that's a hard one! No logic? What's wrong with the American logic, lady?"

"It seems to me," said Cynthia Birch, "that it's a bit illogical—isn't it?—to provide mountains of munitions for Great Britain without sending your young men to use them. Shouldn't they fight with us for civilization—which is as much your concern as ours? Why should we do all the fighting and dying for a civilization which you wish us to defend and which we haven't the strength to defend unless you stand by our side?"

These quiet words seemed to come into this pleasant drawing-room in Massachusetts like a whiff of gas. At least, they seemed to have a stunning effect for a moment. No answer came until the silence was interrupted by a clapping of hands from the doorway in which Penny had been standing listening to Cynthia.

"That's wonderful!" she cried. "Well done, Cynthia! That's exactly what I believe to the innermost cockles of my heart. We ought to be in this war, side by side with the British Armies, Navy, and Air Force. I'm terribly sure we're just lying back behind the shield of the British battleships."

Tiny gave a good-humoured laugh and jeered at his sister.

"Great stuff, Penny! Since you've known that naval guy on H.M.S. *Rodney* you've been singing *Britannia Rules the Waves* all over Massachusetts. I'd like to know what young Brandon thinks about it. I thought I was going to be best man at your wedding."

Penny flung a cushion at her brother's head, but he caught it deftly.

Cynthia Birch left early because of Tessa.

"Oh, I must go," she said, in answer to protestations from Mrs. Hambledon, and Penny's offer to go and sit with Tessa in case she woke up.

Some comments were passed on her by the Hambledons' friends.

"A very odd young woman!" said Robert Hawley Hunt. "I confess she scares me. As cold as a polar she-bear. Very critical, I'd say, of our American way of life."

Mrs. Hunt gave a shrill little laugh.

"Her clothes are deplorable! That frock looked as if it had been in the rag-bag. And fancy coming to an evening party without any stockings. Lack of manners, I call it."

"I guess she has a brain somewhere," remarked Mr. Wakefield. "She put the English case rather well. It gave me a knock when she challenged our logic, though I utterly disagree with everything she said. Still, I must say I admired her frankness. She spoke straight and meant what she said."

"I'm getting to like her," said Mr. Hambledon with his usual good nature. "She's dead honest, and a very good mother."

Penny expressed her own opinion with enthusiasm.

"I think she's marvellous. She's terribly sweet to me, and I like her spirit. It's the spirit of England. She's as English as Stratford-on-Avon."

"Yes, that's what makes her difficult," said Mr. Hunt with a dry smile.

Tiny, sitting back in his chair with his long legs outstretched, did not pass any opinion upon Cynthia Birch.

IV

CYNTHIA WAS ONE of many hundreds of young mothers who had come with their children to the United States when the British Isles were threatened by invasion after the fall of France, and, if they were late in going, as she was, already experiencing the horrors of bombardment from the air. It was the German Blitz over London which had forced her to go, for little Tessa's sake, against all her instincts and all her spirit. She was broken down at last in her refusal to go by the haggard anxiety of her husband—his nerves were in rags and tatters after the first bombs had fallen—and by the endless pleadings of her own father and mother, backed up by her brother and sister.

It began in the flat at Knightsbridge, their private paradise before the war, and now a place of argument and tears and agony because of those black demons overhead.

She remembered a scene when Gerald had come back one evening looking worn out, but with a kind of secret satisfaction in his eyes.

"It's all fixed," he told her. "I've got your exit permit, and the papers for your trip on the Clipper from Lisbon to New York. You'll have to go round and see the American Consul with Tessa."

"I'm not going," she had answered. "I've told you a thousand times, Gerald. Why can't you leave me in peace?"

He stared at her with anger and then laughed in a queer, harsh way.

"Cynthia, you're absurd! You're mad! In peace? Listen! Is that peace?"

The siren was howling the alert. Its rising and falling note was like a banshee, and blood-curdling to frightened souls as Gerald was frightened, not for his own sake, though he hated it, but his wife and child.

"I shan't go to the American Consul," she told him firmly. "I want to stay in England. I want to stay with you. I don't believe in running away."

Gerald threw up his hands. His thin, delicate-looking face became paler. Little lines appeared about his mouth and eyes.

"You're an unnatural mother," he cried. "Cynthia, my darling, we've had this out so often. For God's sake, don't let us go through it all over again. Don't you want to save Tessa's life? Do you want me to see you both torn to pieces by flying steel, or buried under an avalanche of masonry? Hark at these devils now!"

Cynthia listened and saw Gerald listening intently. All his nerves were racked. She could see fear in his eyes. Somewhere in London there were heavy bangs and crashes. The floor-boards under their blue carpet trembled with a kind of earthquake tremor.

"It's a long way off," she said quietly. "Somewhere in the East End."

He came and put his arms about her.

"Cynthia, dearest heart, answer my question. Do you want to see Tessa killed? I know your own courage. I wish I had a share of it, but for Tessa's sake and for my peace of mind I implore you to take this chance of escape. In a few days it may be too late."

She unloosed his arms about her and went towards the mantelpiece with wet eyes and a queer sharp pain in her heart. She would have to yield, she supposed. Everybody was trying to push her out of England. They were talking about duty and self-sacrifice and motherly love and all that. They seemed to think that Tessa was the only person in the world.

She turned round to him, she remembered, and spoke in a cold voice:

"I suppose I'll have to go. You're all so terrified about Tessa. You don't care a damn about me. Tessa's life is not more valuable than all the millions of children who will have to stay in England. Why shouldn't she take her chance with them? If she gets killed she won't be the only one. Don't you realize, Gerald, that if I go it will be a long divorce between you and me? The war is going to last for years. How am I going to endure the exile? Didn't you and I swear to stay by each other for better or worse until death do us part? I shall fall in love with somebody else—I warn you! Some kinky-haired American. That's the price you'll have to pay for getting rid of me. We shall never see each other again. Still, I suppose I'll have to go."

It was not in her character to talk like that. Generally she kept pretty sane and level-headed. Tonight she felt a little mad. She hated the idea of leaving England. She wanted to stay with this nervous, terror-stricken husband who adored her and to whom she had given her body and soul.

That night had been a bad one in London. Gerald had insisted upon her going down with him to the basement. Most of the people from the other flats in this big block of flats had gone down—young women in dressing-gowns over their pyjamas, and bare feet in loose slippers, young husbands and wives like Gerald and Cynthia with sleepy children wrapped up in blankets; elderly women who spoke with forced gaiety in high strident voices; a famous poet, tall and silent and melancholy; a few officers in uniform; an old Admiral on the retired list—cherubic-looking in his dressing-gown, with ruffled hair; one of the Talks Directors on the B.B.C. They sat around on the floor, or stood against the walls smoking cigarettes, chatting cheerfully, refusing to show the white feather, though every now and again they felt that earth tremor and heard heavy explosions.

"A great nuisance, these things!" said one of the elderly men. "What good does Hitler think it does him?"

"Most annoying," agreed one of the elderly ladies. "I resent being forced out of my bed."

"I confess it frightens me very much," said one of the officers in uniform who did not look at all scared. "I'm entirely unheroic. I should like to be in a very deep shelter sixty feet below the ground."

"To hell with Hitler!" said one of the young wives, who was smoking a cigarette through a long holder. "I wish we had a drink down here."

"I'll go and fetch you one," volunteered a young man in a blue silk dressing-gown with golden dragons emblazoned upon it.

"No, no, don't risk your young life for a spot of alcohol. I can hold out till the All Clear."

Cynthia nodded to one or two of these people and passed a few words with them.

"They are going to stay in England," she thought. "I'm being sent into exile. I want to share the risks with them. If they are going to be killed, I'd like to be killed with them. But I wouldn't like Tessa to be killed—dear little Tessa who doesn't know anything about all this. I was a fool to talk like that to Gerald. It wasn't quite true. I should break my heart if anything happened to Tessa."

Gerald was talking to a group of friends. He was talking quite cheerfully and without that look of haggard anxiety. He was like that among people. It was only when he was alone with her that he revealed his fears.

There were more dull crashes. After one of them the basement floor of solid cement seemed to rise a little and then subside.

"It's all hell in London tonight," said one of the officers.

She nodded and answered him.

"I'd like to have a look at it. Come up on the roof with me."

Captain Baskerville raised his eyebrows and smiled.

"A bit risky, isn't it? Still, if you feel like it—"

They went together to the top floor by lift and then up an iron ladder to the flat roof—from which there was a wonderful view of London, beautiful and terrible that night. The sky was rose-coloured, its whole dome filled with pulsating light. Above many fires, north and east and south, it was blood-red with a seething moving red into which tongues of flame leapt up. Great buildings were blazing fiercely and sending up showers of sparks and scarlet-coloured smoke. Eastwards, there was a dome high above all other buildings, touched by a crimson glow, and looking engulfed in fire. It was the dome of St. Paul's.

"It's a hellish sight," said Captain Baskerville in a low voice. "It makes me shudder. London! Who would believe it in this twentieth century of so-called civilization?"

"I'm glad I came up," said Cynthia. "One ought to see this thing."

She leaned with her elbows on a stone parapet, her chin on her clasped hands, staring at this inferno which was London. She had been born here. She had played with her toys in Kensington Gardens. As a young girl she had been to the Tower of London and many times to St. Paul's. She and Gerald, and a group of friends, had dined and laughed and talked nonsense in many little restaurants from Sloane Square to Soho. She had danced in the Café de Paris. She had said her prayers in Old Chelsea Church. She had walked with Gerald through the Middle Temple Gardens. London was in her spirit and in her bones. Now, below her, London was on fire and its people were being killed amidst the ruins. She gave a hard dry sob and put her hands over her eyes for a moment.

"Let's go down," she said after that. "Gerald will miss me and think I'm dead."

It was in the autumn that she flew to Lisbon with Tessa and said good-bye in her heart to England, hating to go.

Gerald had pulled strings. There had been innumerable delays, during which she had fled to the country with Tessa, staying at her father's house outside the village of Cranleigh. Night after night she heard the German bombers on their way to London, and while Tessa was asleep went into the garden to watch the searchlights peering about the sky and trying to catch one of those black-winged demons in their long fingers of light. Guns were firing from the outer defences of London, somewhere about Epsom and Reigate and Newlands Corner. She could see the flash of their shell-bursts glittering like star-dust. Far away—forty miles away—the sky was glowing crimson where new fires were started and more ruin was being made. Thousands of people would be in the shelters, leading that queer underground life to which civilization had come. Many more—old maids, like her aunts, Millicent and Betty—would be sitting under their stairs in little houses in the London suburbs, afraid and yet heroic.

Under the stairs, poor dears, in little houses which fell into heaps of rubble and splintered wood under high-explosive shells.

Her father stood by her side sometimes in the garden when she went out to look at the searchlights. He spoke gravely and sometimes bitterly. "All this is an outrage against Christian civilization. . . . We're being led back to the jungle. . . . Science has betrayed humanity. I would kill all the scientists. . . . This ought never to have happened. We all share the guilt. . . . If we had been wiser Hitler would never have arrived. . . . I shall be glad, old girl, when you and Tessa are winging your way to the United States, out of all this to a land of peace."

"I would rather stay, Father," answered Cynthia.

One night in the garden she had a fright. Many German bombs had fallen round about in this countryside, mostly on heaths and commons. They had been released by German pilots chased by our fighters and discarding their loads anywhere. Several times this old country house had been shaken by explosions. Its old timbers had quivered. Once when she was playing billiards with her father the table rose, the balls ran about, and there were seven bangs—a stick of bombs—less than half a mile away.

"Unpleasantly close," said her father. "It spoilt my break."

But that night in the garden, less than half a mile away, something happened. It seemed to be just over their heads. It was a screaming bomb. It gave a kind of gobbling shriek like some laughing devil as it spiralled down.

Cynthia felt her father clutch her. He dragged her down into some rhododendron bushes where they fell together in a huddle.

"Sorry, old girl!" he said, after the bomb had exploded only a field away.

She picked herself up, with a torn dress and many scratches, and then laughed.

"I thought I was dead that time, Daddy. A near miss!"

Another sound startled her. Through an open window under one of the gables came a child's screams.

"Oh, poor mite!" cried Cynthia, making a rush for the house. It was Tessa, frightened for the first time by the noise of war.

That was a week before she left England.

Gerald broke down the night before she went. They both wept. This war was tearing them apart, perhaps for years. They might never see each other again, or if they saw each other again they might both be changed. In any case, this love of theirs was now a torture to them because of this sword cutting them in half.

"Thank God you and Tessa will be safe when you're once across the Atlantic," said Gerald, with his arms about her. "No war over there! No bombs. No black-out. . . ."

"Why should I leave you here?" cried Cynthia. "It's idiotic. I shan't go. I shall tear up all those tickets. You're not fit to be left alone. You're C3 and need a nurse. You're always in a state of nerves. I shall stay and take care of you. Oh, my darling, let me stay and be with you whatever happens!"

Gerald was unfit for any branch of military service because of a delicate physique, but strong enough to carry on as a barrister in the Middle Temple. She saw his pale face as he took off his hat and waved to her when she carried Tessa into the aeroplane bound for Lisbon. He had kissed Tessa a hundred times that morning. It was hardest for him to part from Tessa, whom he worshipped.

Presently, as the engines roared, and the plane taxied round the aerodrome and rose above the earth, Gerald became a black dot among a lot of other black dots on the edge of a flat field.

"When shall we see Daddy again?" asked Tessa. "Tomorrow?"

"Oh, quite soon, I hope," said Cynthia brightly.

V

Cynthia was not ungrateful to these American friends who heaped her with kindness in Massachusetts. The Hambledons, the Hunts, the Wakefields, the Zimmermanns, and many others were all very nice and generous. She came to have a special liking and admiration for Penny, so vital, so high-spirited, and so flamingly pro-English. It was good to see her riding towards the cottage on her brown mare with the white socks, as graceful as a young Amazon and as pretty as a picture. Mr. and Mrs. Hambledon were kindness itself. But as the months passed and then a winter—the hard winter of Massachusetts—dropping to twenty below zero, and then another spring and another summer, she knew perfectly well that she was not making good among these people. They had a query in their minds about her. She had been dropped by the Zimmermanns, who never invited her now, and did not come round to the cottage, as once they did, with books and magazines and other gifts. She tried to think how she could have offended them. Perhaps she had been too abrupt in her expressions of opinion. Perhaps now and then she had been critical of little things in the American way of life which mostly she admired—the frightful amount of advertising on the radio which interrupted the news of war in Europe with its death and agony to recommend a hair tonic, or a brand of cigars, or a new flavour in chewing gum with false and sickening emotion. She had made fun of that one evening. It hadn't gone down too well. The Americans, she found, were very sensitive about any kind of criticism from any English person. They regarded it as English "edge" or English snobbishness, through they were highly critical of themselves. But that was not the only cause of her being a social disappointment to them. She was too careless, of course, about her clothes. She hated dressing up in smart frocks, and in any case she hadn't brought over smart frocks. She went about like a gipsy, with bare legs. They didn't mind that, perhaps, during the day, but they expected her to turn up decently clad at their evening parties. Perhaps she had been careless about that, having rushed round after putting Tessa to bed, and arriving late for the same reason, with untidy hair—it refused to be tidy—and her little black frock over which Tessa had been sick so that it had left a stain.

Penny and Mrs. Hambledon had given her some frocks, but somehow she didn't feel happy in them, and didn't have time to put them on as often as she ought to have done. Little things like that. Many little things all adding up. Hot words in defence of British rule in India, of which she knew very little, except what she had heard from her father; a refusal to admit that English slums were worse than New York slums which she had never seen; that argument about American duty to defend civilization by the side of Great Britain. A remark that English villages were more beautiful than American villages, or small towns, which was true, she thought. She didn't want to criticize but she had to defend England when it was attacked, even finding herself defending Mr. Chamberlain's policy of appeasement at Munich. That didn't go down well either. But there was something more than this, more irritating to these American friends, because they thought that she didn't like them, and didn't like the American way of life, which was untrue. It was her resistance to the social whirl, her refusal of innumerable invitations, excuses too often repeated because she could not join their cocktail parties, or their expeditions in search of amusement as far as Boston. How could she join them? Tessa needed constant attention, being delicate and not yet hardened to this climate of extremes. A Portuguese girl, Paula, came in for a few hours each day and sometimes would sit with Tessa in the evenings, but this old eighteenth-century frame-house, not fitted up with labour-saving gadgets, necessitated a lot of cleaning. There was the furnace to be stoked—a hellish business in winter and almost one man's job. There was the washing to be done—Tessa's little clothes. She had to go shopping in Taunton three times a week as nothing was delivered. It was all very difficult and all very tiring. But in any case—she had to be fair—she shirked too much social stuff. She wanted to be alone a good deal, with her own thoughts. She had always been the cat that walked alone. Gerald had accused her of that. She wanted to read every scrap about the war in the *New York Times*. She wanted to hear the news over the radio, though it tore her heart out because it was nearly all bad. She wanted to read fairy-tales to Tessa and draw little pictures for her. She wanted to read her own books. She wanted to walk alone among the silver birches by the lake when Paula was playing with Tessa. She had always been bewildered and worried in a crowd of people, and the Americans like to get together too much, she thought. They were always getting together. They wanted her to come in with them. Even before breakfast the telephone-bell started ringing.

"Is that Mrs. Birch? Oh, good-morning, Mrs. Birch! How's Tessa? We're making up a little party for a symphony concert in Boston. Some British naval officers from the *Rodney* are coming. Do join us, won't you? We'll fetch you in the car. Now don't say no!"

She said "No," not always, but perhaps too often, to invitations of this kind. They didn't seem to understand how busy she was. They didn't understand that she liked solitude.

Well, she had quite a lot of it in the winter. The Hambledons, the Wakefields, and the Hunts went back to their houses in Boston, only coming back for Christmas and occasional week-ends. The countryside was deep in snow, and the great lake of Assawampsett, to which her cottage garden went down, was covered with ice a foot deep. Village boys skated on it and their shouts and laughter was good company in this white solitude which she preferred to the Hambledons' big house on Commonwealth Avenue, Boston, where she and Tessa stayed for several weeks. Then she had to take her place at big dinner-parties, and go to Symphony concerts and leave Tessa in the care of Mrs. Hambledon's maids. It was jolly in a way. There were plenty of young people, all very vivacious, all getting engaged, or breaking-off engagements, or getting married. But she was not good at dinner-table conversation and became rather tired of the constant and passionate discussion about President Roosevelt, whose name was anathema to some of these women—they called him "That Man"—and an almost God-like hero to the rebels against Republican tradition. But in her secret mind she was always in exile. She was always a refugee. Her heart was in England. Her spirit fled to it halfway through a dinner-table conversation so that she dropped into silence and became deeply absent-minded. What was she doing here anyway at this table, laden with rich food, while in England her own folk were on short rations—two ounces of butter a week, one and twopence worth of meat a week—about two chops—just a drip of milk, according to Gerald. Gerald wrote, every week, long letters full of detail, sometimes snipped out by the censor, and often a long time in coming because of the U-boats, or the erratic delivery by air mail. The Middle Temple Hall was down. Chelsea Old Church had been blasted into rubble. St. Peter's, Eaton Square, where they were married, had been badly hit. His brother Frank had been killed in Lybia. He had had a bad dose of influenza. Everybody was down with it. The war wasn't going too well. The Germans were committing every kind of atrocity in Poland. London was getting shabby and battered, though they were tidying up the ruins. He had gone for a walk up Bond Street. Most of its shops were boarded up. Round St. Paul's it was like a scene in Ypres.

"I don't believe you heard what I was saying, Mrs. Birch!" remarked a young Harvard professor who was sitting next to her, and had been telling her a long story which was probably amusing.

"I'm so sorry," she told him. "My thoughts were wandering."

They thought she was suffering from English coldness and languid boredom. She was only suffering from the sense of exile. She was only tortured by it.

Winter jumped into Spring suddenly and brilliantly. Spring gave a warm clasp to Summer hot in its embrace, burning hot on the Hambledons' golf-course, and down by the lake which shone like burnished metal. The first Hambledon to appear from Boston was that very tall young man, Tiny, who took up his quarters in the old mill-house. He had become a friend of hers. For some reason he seemed to like her company, and certainly she liked his. He was restful in a way, and helpful as a handy-man, and very sweet to Tessa. He could endure long silences if neither of them were inclined to talk, and had a habit of stretching himself at great length on the floor in front of her fireplace with his eyes closed. He was keen on music, and tuned up an old piano in the cottage so that she could play to him. During the winter he had come over from Boston for week-ends, and at Christmas had spent a month in his mill-house absorbed in a new play, but finding time, good-naturedly, to come over and give her a hand in stoking the old furnace—that black devil of a thing which had to be raked out each morning—raising suffocating clouds of white dust, and then heaped up with coal lest they should perish with cold. He did some tobogganning with them, and she trusted his strength and skill, even with Tessa, hurtling down a steep hill.

Now in the Spring, before the family had come, he came striding down to the cottage after lunch and after his morning's work, and suggested a picnic tea in the woods up by the Big Stone upon which in the old days Red Indians had carved totem signs, and sat in Red Indian silence staring out across the waters of the great lake. They walked through silver birches, whose broken branches, snapped off by winter's frost, lay strewn across the track. Tiny carried Tessa shoulder high with a kettle in his other hand. He was good at making a wood fire under the shelter of the Big Stone. He was amusing in his quiet, grave way, and pleasant company because he didn't talk too much, too often.

But he could talk. Sometimes after those silences, stretched out on the carpet, he would sit up and give tongue. He talked sometimes about his "kid brother," Edward, who had gone and lost himself in France.

"He's playing some queer game over there. He used to be in love with a Russian girl called Olga. In some of his letters to me, not meant for family reading, he indulged in romantic lunacy about her. Then he seems to have cooled off. Lately, in the rare letters which come from him, he speaks of a girl called Lucile de Rollencourt, but rather guardedly. He seems to be living in an old farmhouse with her family. But he moves about France and gets back to Paris sometimes. Now and then he cables for quite a stiff number of bucks, which worries my father, though he can well afford to send them. I have an idea that he's up to his neck in the French underground movement. Maybe he's asking to get shot against a white wall. Silly, I call it."

"Why?" asked Cynthia.

"He's a perfectly good American. Why risk one's life for those lousy French?"

"Are they lousy?"

"Lousy in a metaphorical sense, dear lady. Essentially corrupt. Rotten. That's to say, lousy."

He had never been to France, she understood.

Sometimes he talked about war. In fact, that was a theme which cropped up frequently. He hated war. He had written a play about it. It was now running on Broadway, ridiculing the whole damn business of war, and the way in which the peoples let themselves be fooled by politicians playing power-politics, and appealing to their patriotism, and doping them with false old slogans which made suckers of the mob, who became the victims and the gun-fodder.

"We ought to get rid of patriotism. Didn't your Dr. Johnson say it was the last refuge of the scoundrel? Didn't your Nurse Cavell say, on the eve of her execution, 'Patriotism is not enough'?"

"Wouldn't you fight for the United States?" asked Cynthia.

"No, sir!" answered Tiny, that young giant of America.

"It's the business of our leaders to keep the United States out of war. That's what they're there for. Nobody is going to attack us. We're three thousand miles away from European quarrels and vendettas. Let us keep three thousand miles away. We've built up a pretty good civilization, haven't we? Lots of black spots in it, a hell of a lot of iniquity, graft, and corruption in high places and low, cruelties and intolerances here and there, gangsters and gunmen here and there. Yes, I know all that; but, broadly speaking, we people have liberty, a high standard of living, and a decent chance of education. That is to say, we're getting civilized. We're leading the way in putting the good things of life in reach of the ordinary fellow and the girl in the coffee-shop. We're reaching out, some of us, to art and beauty. It's no longer the prerogative of Europe. Our builders have imagination and audacity and play with steel. We have some pretty good writers, turning out fine stuff, some of 'em. We can do without Europe. We're raising our standards and groping forward to something mighty big and something mighty fine. Our flowering time, I guess. Why not, when we have every strain of every race, and opportunity for any guy who has a touch of genius? We're a kindly folk, seems to me. We don't want to go murdering on the big scale. Our emigrants came here to find peace.

Is that swindling Messiah who calls himself Roosevelt going to spoil it all by leading us back to the European battlefields? He's playing up for it. Well, he won't get me, lady. I'm telling you."

That was quite a long monologue for a strong, silent man.

"You're talking stuff and nonsense," she told him.

"I'm talking God's own truth," he assured her.

They had long arguments on this subject, a kind of continuous duel or debate which cropped up at odd times, but was not too prolonged at any one sitting.

He thought England had made a mess of things. British statesmen had fallen between two stools. Either they should have re-armed when Germany re-armed, or they should not have declared war when they were too weak to fight it. They had guaranteed Poland and other little nations—bloody-minded little nations—when they couldn't have guaranteed the life of a louse in a peasant's shirt.

"It was midsummer madness when old Chamberlain revoked," said Tiny Hambledon. "He ought to have refused to go to war to appease the clamour of Labour members who had voted against armaments."

"Hitler would have turned on us," said Cynthia. "He would have crushed all Europe and then turned upon our little island. Don't you see that, big man?"

The big man didn't see it.

"According to extracts from *Mein Kampf*—I can't say I've read more than that, and don't want to—he expresses an admiration for the British Empire. You could have made a deal with him."

"Never!" said Cynthia. "He's out for world domination. One day he'll want the United States or Latin America. Then you'll have to fight him."

"I'm not going to fight anybody," answered Tiny Hambledon. "I shall learn German. If the Germans come here I shall talk to them politely. They'll soon lose themselves in our Melting Pot. They make very good settlers."

"Haven't you any pride, Mr. Hambledon, sir?" asked Cynthia. "Have you a coward heart? Are you afraid to die?"

"Sure I am," he answered frankly, "and sure I haven't any false pride. I'm a follower of Jesus Christ, though no good Christian. I believe in passive resistance, which was the strength of the Christian martyrs who captured the world with it. If they had taken to the sword they would have perished by the sword."

Cynthia smiled at him for this argument about the early Christians. Often he spoke in a way which would have shocked any English churchgoer. Presently she answered seriously:

"I agree with you about war, Tiny. Who doesn't—at least in England? We went to the ultimate limits of honour to avoid war, but we couldn't let the other peoples get trampled down and made into slaves. We had to fight Hitler and his gangsters or lose our soul. One has to fight devilry."

Tiny shook his head and waved her argument away with one of his big hands.

"One becomes a devil oneself when one starts fighting. It's only a competition in mass murder. More and bigger bombs. You kill my children and I'll kill yours, and also your mothers and sisters, and aunts and cousins. You destroy my cities and I'll blast yours off the face of the earth. What a game! What a beautiful ideal for civilized humanity! To hell with it! Play something, Cynthia. Play *Drink to me only with thine eyes*, and some of the old songs."

He read out some of his plays to her, and she found them interesting, but rather queer, with a grim and satirical spirit. The one about war was having a success on Broadway.

Once she asked him an abrupt question in her straight, candid way.

"Why do you spend so much time with me? Why do you read out your work as if my opinion mattered at all?"

He was rather staggered by that frankness of enquiry. He looked at her and laughed uneasily before answering.

"Lady, I like you! I have a respect for your intelligence. I find I can discuss things with you in a reasonable way—quite impossible with the crowd in Boston or even in New York. You don't get all het up if you don't agree with me, as mostly you don't. And in any case—" he hesitated, and did not finish that sentence.

"Yes?" she asked.

"In any case," he said, "I'm a sentimental cuss. I want a woman's friendship. I'd be glad to think I've found it."

She fluttered her eyelids and smiled at him a little shyly.

"You've found it all right," she said. "But don't make it sentimental. I hate sentimentality."

"What you say goes with me," he answered.

Mrs. Hambledon's face paled slightly, and there was distress in her eyes.

"I don't know that I like knowing it," she answered. "It makes me scared about him."

"Tell us, Chas," said Mr. Hunt quietly.

"We're dying to know," said Penny, clasping her bare knees.

"Well, then, it's like this: Your Edward is caught up in the French underground movement of resistance. He's one of the agents in a secret chain working for the escape of prisoners of war and young Frenchmen trying to get to England to join General de Gaulle. He's a faker of passports. He forges rubber stamps of Vichy. He repaints photographs, putting on beards and taking them off. He draws caricatures for the underground Press. He travels about France on his American papers as a liaison officer between the secret groups. He lives with a family on the border line between the Occupied and Unoccupied zones. They receive the refugees and pass them on to friends in the unoccupied region. He's up to his neck in all that, and wants to drag me into it; but I'm not having any. No, sir!"

"We guessed something of the sort," remarked Tiny. "I've long thought that my kid brother was quite crazy. Now I know."

"I'm proud of him!" cried Penny excitedly. "I think he's wonderful. I have a hero for a brother."

"You have a damn fool for a brother," said Tiny angrily. "And he has a damn little fool for a sister."

"It's very alarming," said Mrs. Hambledon gravely.

"There's nothing we can do about it, I'm afraid," said Mr. Hambledon, looking very worried.

Chas Hunt had other details to tell. He described his adventure with Edward before the Germans entered Paris, and their meeting with a young French officer named Armand de Rollencourt. That had been the beginning of the trouble. It was this officer who had invited Edward to drive to his old farmhouse near Tours with an English captain who had been wounded and couldn't walk. Armand de Rollencourt had a sister called Lucile. It was quite obvious from one or two things let drop by Edward that he was pretty far gone in love with her. She was one of those French girls who hated the Vichy Government and was ready to risk death for de Gaulle.

"I guess she's right," said Penny.

Chas Hunt thought she was wrong. Partly wrong at least. There were a lot of traitors and scoundrels at Vichy. But in his view old Pétain was playing a game of cat and mouse with Hitler. At least, he was holding on to the French Fleet and keeping his North African Empire out of German control. In his judgment the United States were wise in keeping touch with Vichy. One day it might be valuable, this liaison.

"What in hell have we to do with all that?" asked Tiny, who lay at full length in the sun with his hands clasped under his head. "Let's keep out of it."

"Let's get back to Edward," suggested Mrs. Hambledon. "I thought he was in love with a girl called Olga. A Russian girl in Paris. She seemed very charming, according to what he wrote about her."

Chas Hunt laughed, and then remembered something.

"Jeepers Creepers! I nearly forgot to tell you about that. That girl Olga—I know her well—is coming to Boston next week, if she's still travelling around with a Jewish guy who plays the piano like Paderewski. Paul Simon. She chucked Edward in order to cherish this sick genius. Married him, I believe. He's a master at Chopin. He used to play to us when I threw a party in my apartment in Paris. He used to ravish our souls."

"Sure you have a soul, buddy?" asked Tiny. "Does a newspaper man find any use for a soul?"

Chas Hunt took this irony good-humouredly.

"If newspaper men had had the running of this world," he said, "it would be a pretty good place. We're the fellows who know."

He talked a lot more about Edward. It was all very alarming to Edward's father and mother.

VII

IT WAS WITH Chas Hunt that they went to hear Paul Simon in Boston —Tiny and Penny with their father and mother.

Tiny found the seat in the concert hall uncomfortable for his long legs, but forgot that discomfort when he listened to a pianist who played Chopin with a miraculous touch. A queer-looking guy, he thought, as Simon came on to the platform in a shiny black suit rather too short in the sleeves, and with hair which wanted cutting. He looked ill and emaciated, and was a good advertisement for starving France, though he had left Paris before it began to starve. Distinctly a Jew, thought Tiny Hambledon, but with a fine delicate face like a Jewish scholar or prophet. He took no notice at all of the applause which greeted him, mostly from an audience of women. Perhaps some of them had heard him before, but the blurb on the programme had told them that he was recognized as the finest exponent of Chopin's genius in Europe. In fact, his agents went further details about life in France, some of them amusing, and some tragic. It was all very interesting. But at one minute to nine Cynthia looked at her wrist-watch. She didn't want to miss the nine o'clock news.

Tiny, who had kept his eyes on her, grinned and asked a question:

"Must we?"

Without waiting for an answer he slouched across the room—this big cool room with its open windows looking across the golf-course to the lake of Assawampsett—and switched on the radio. He knew that Cynthia Birch hungered for news almost morbidly.

The others went on talking until suddenly something startled them. Perhaps it was Chas Hunt's break in his monologue, and his sudden exclamation:

"Jeepers Creepers!"

The American radio commentator and news man was giving out portentous words—on this twenty-second of June.

"At three o'clock this morning the Germans invaded Russia along a vast front reaching from the Baltic to the Black Sea. . . . Hitler has issued a proclamation to the German nation saying that after being condemned for a month to keep silence he can now speak openly. He asserts that Russia was contemplating an attack on Germany in violation of their pact of friendship. The German radio propagandists are telling the German people that great battles lie ahead. 'Down with Stalin! Down with the Jews and the exploiters!' "

Chas Hunt stood up from his chair, knocking over his glass without noticing it. He was excited.

"Hitler has gone mad," he said. "Did I say gone mad? He ought to have been put into an asylum years ago. This is a proof of it."

Cynthia also stood up from her chair. Tiny Hambledon watched her curiously, wondering why she had a look on her face like Joan of Arc listening to the voices.

"It's good luck for England," she said. "He can't turn all his strength against us now."

"Will the Russians be able to put up any resistance?" asked Mr. Hambledon. "They didn't make much of a show in World War I."

Chas Hunt thought they were better prepared than most people knew. One of his colleagues in Moscow had passed through France and Hunt had had a talk with him. He said that Russia had been forging a tremendous war machine, and training a vast army behind a screen of secrecy. There was a new spirit in Russia. They would fight to the death against this German invasion. That's what his friend had said, and he was a fellow of sound judgment.

Cynthia was listening again to the radio.

"Mr. Churchill," said the speaker, "has just broadcast to the British people. The following is a summary which has just reached us."

"Shall we listen?" asked Cynthia, as a hint to those who were talking.

"Oh, God!" said Tiny Hambledon in a low voice. "How long, Oh, Lord, how long?"

But with the others he listened.

"Mr. Churchill says that he gave Stalin warning of the German attack, and he hopes that it did not fall unheeded. He withdraws nothing that he ever said against Communism, but all that fades away before the spectacle which is now unfolding. . . ."

"I see the Russian soldiers," said Mr. Churchill, "standing on the threshold of their nation's land, guarding the fields their fathers have tilled from time immemorial. . . . I see the ten thousand villages of Russia, where the means of existence are wrung so hardly from the soil, but where there are still primordial human joys, where maidens laugh and children play. . . . But now I have to declare the policy of His Majesty's Government, and I feel it is a decision in which the great Dominions will in due course concur. But we must speak it now, without a day's delay. We have but one aim and one single irrevocable purpose. We are resolved to destroy Hitler and every vestige of the Nazi régime. From this nothing will turn us—nothing. We will never parley, we will never negotiate, with Hitler or any of his gang. Any man or State who fights against Nazism will have our aid. Any man or State who marches with Hitler is our foe. . . . It follows, therefore, that we shall give whatever help we can to Russia and the Russian people. . . . We have already offered to the Government of Soviet Russia any technical or economic assistance which is in our power."

"Well, it's great news," said Mrs. Hambledon.

"England no longer stands alone." Cynthia spoke with suppressed emotion. "It was too much for us alone."

"That man, Churchill," said Chas Hunt, "is a great guy. I'll say that England is lucky in having him."

Tiny Hambledon seemed to be suffering some unfavourable reaction to Mr. Churchill's speech.

"Cripes!" he said. "It makes me laugh."

"What makes you laugh?" asked Cynthia, smiling over to him.

Tiny raised his long legs and clasped his knees.

"The darned hypocrisy of it all," he answered. "I thought little old England was fighting for liberty and democracy. That's what I've always been told. That's what Mr. Roosevelt keeps on telling us. That's what all those lousy correspondents keep on putting over the radio. 'This war is in defence of the world's liberty and future civilization,' says Winston

Churchill in noble words, which melt the heart of the American public as well as his own."

"What's wrong with that?" asked Cynthia, with a challenging look at this long-limbed young man.

"Why, dammit," he answered angrily, "that noble fellow Churchill now gives his blessing and offers all aid to the greatest enemy of liberty and democracy on God's earth, not excepting Adolf Hitler. Stalin is autocrat of the autocrats. All his people are robots under his iron tyranny. There's no more difference between a Communist and a Nazi than between one louse and another. They're just as ruthless. One has its Gestapo and the other its Ogpu. Both have their tortures. Both subordinate the liberty of the individual to the interest of the State. That is to say, both peoples are slaves to the ruffians at the top. The individual soul ain't worth a dime. Now Russia becomes the noble Ally of that liberty-loving people, the English, who like other people to fight their battles and do a hell of a lot of propaganda over here with the same idea—which won't come off this time. No, sir!"

Cynthia looked him in the eyes and her face flushed.

"I'm English," she said. "I don't like to hear England insulted."

She rose from her chair and moved towards the door.

For a moment there was silence and then Penny made a rush at her.

"No, Cynthia, don't go! Tiny has gone crazy. He's perfectly crazy when he talks about the war. He makes me mad."

"That's all right," said Cynthia. "But I must be going anyhow."

She insisted upon going.

"Now you've offended a beautiful lady," said Chas Hunt, with a laugh at Tiny Hambledon.

That tall young man answered the laugh uneasily.

"I guess I hurt her feelings. I'm sorry."

He flung a lighted cigarette into the fireplace.

"I ought to have left out that bit about England," he said. "The blood went to my head over Churchill's speech."

"What was wrong with it?" asked Chas Hunt. "None of us like Russian Communism, but this attack on Russia is a godsend to England, and personally I'm all for little old England. They've shown that they have guts. The way they've stood up to the Blitz is one of the heroic chapters of mankind. And they wouldn't show the white flag after Dunkirk when France collapsed, and when they had just nothing except their old tradition, and a Home Guard without rifles, and a bunch of boys in the Air Force who knocked hell out of the *Luftwaffe*."

"And the Royal Navy," added Penny, "hunting down the U-boats, and keeping the freedom of the seas for us as well as themselves."

Tiny Hambledon laughed again, but without good humour.

"That's all right. I've nothing against England except a secret conviction that she'll get us into this war somehow. And I'm against war. I'm against the whole bloody business of war. It's uncivilized. It's just old-fashioned murder on the grand scale. I want to keep out of it. I want this country to keep out of it. I believe in art, and music, and education, and the right of the individual to do what he damn well likes without being rounded up for gun fodder."

"Buddy," said Penny, "you talk like a long-haired high-brow in Greenwich Village. What you say is just lousy. And you've offended Cynthia Birch so that she won't speak to you again."

"Oh, hell!" said Tiny. He kicked a hassock out of his way and strode out of the room with a dark look in his eyes.

"There's something in what he says," said Mr. Hambledon, who had not interrupted this family argument. "I'm getting scared about Mr. Roosevelt's foreign policy. Step by step—this Lease-Lend business—he's drifting towards intervention in the European War. I have two sons. I don't want them to spill their blood in foreign fields. Edward has gone already. I've lost him, haven't I?"

"Now then, Pop," said Penny, "don't shed tears over Edward. He's the only member of the family who shows a spark of heroism. We ought to be fighting by England's side. We're just behaving like selfish cowards, cheering on England from the side lines."

"Penny," cried Mrs. Hambledon, "you're very wild. Don't speak so wildly."

"Don't be so Bostonian, Mother," answered Penny.

Chas Hunt gave a loud and good-natured laugh.

"Say, this is quite an exciting evening. I'm having an interesting time, I'll say I am. What about another spot of gin and lime?"

It was a very warm evening.

IX

PENELOPE HAMBLEDON WAS not a wild young woman, but she was certainly not Bostonian as she had accused her mother of being, unjustly as it happened, because Mrs. Hambledon had revolted from the Back Bay tradition of ultra-conservatism, and was considered to be almost "Red" in her political opinions.

But Penelope was in what she called a "jam." It was due to an historical incident in naval history. H.M.S. *Rodney* of the British Navy had put into Boston harbour for repairs after being knocked about in action against a German pocket-battleship. The Bostonians had offered unbounded hospitality to the officers and men, although a certain amount of fighting occurred between American seamen and British Jack Tars according to ancient tradition. They were entertained lavishly at public banquets and private dinner-tables. It was at a private dinner-party in the Boston house of Mr. and Mrs. Wakefield that Penny first met Richard Arkwright of the *Rodney*, whom she found almost too emotionally attractive. He had very blue eyes and very fair hair, and his face, she thought, was beautiful and heroic like one of King Arthur's knights—Lancelot, or Gawaine, in Tennyson's *Idylls of the King*, which she had read as a college girl.

They sat next to each other at Mr. Wakefield's table.

"Are you being well treated in the United States?" she enquired.

His blue eyes smiled at her. She noticed how deeply blue they were.

"Rather! I should say we are. You're giving us a wonderful time. We can't compete with American hospitality."

"How do you like Boston?"

He liked it enormously. Parts of it reminded him of Kensington where he had been born. Only there was more of it. He thought it a fine city.

"Something happened here once," he said, "which strained relations between England and America. Wasn't there a Boston tea-party? I seem to remember."

"Your memory is not at fault," she told him, answering his smile. "It was a regrettable incident. It led to war between us."

"Yes," said this naval lieutenant, who had camouflaged his knowledge of history. "You gave us an awful licking. I seem to remember that."

"Does it still rankle?" asked Penny, with a light laugh.

"Not in the least," he assured her. "There's a statue to George Washington outside our National Gallery. It was a kind of Civil War really. Washington was a typical English country gentleman. The American colonists of that time were all of British or Scottish or Irish stock. Isn't that so?"

"I guess you're right," said Penny. "Have you ever read a book called *Oliver Wiswell?* It gives the Tory point of view. Anyhow, it was a long way back. We've forgotten the Ancient Grudge. We had a few prejudices left before the beginning of this war, but now most of us are very proud if we have a drop of English blood in us. England has been terribly heroic."

"It's nice of you to say so," said Richard Arkwright of the *Rodney*.

"We ought to be in this war with you," said Penny. "It's our war as well as yours. I mean, that it ought to be if we believe in liberty and democracy, as we mostly do."

He glanced sideways at her, and she saw a glint of humour in his blue eyes.

"You're the first American I've heard say such a thing," he told her. "I'm jolly glad to hear it."

He put down his knife and fork for a moment and spoke in a low voice which had a kind of thrill in it.

"If you were in with us we could finish off this fellow Hitler pretty quick. We're a bit overstrained at the moment. You've no idea of the pull on the poor old British Navy, to say nothing of the Merchant Service, which is doing grand work without glory and on damn bad pay. I could tell you something about that."

"Tell me," asked Penny. "I'd just be thrilled to hear it."

She was thrilled by some of the stories he told her about the hunting down of U-boats and the fight put up by the little ships against torpedo attacks, dive-bombers, surface-raiders, and magnetic mines. Some of the convoys to Malta had gone through hell fire, but some of them had got there—and did it again.

Presently he checked himself and laughed shyly.

"I say, I've been boring you no end! And it sounds as though I were bucking about the British Navy! Sorry!"

"You've been giving me a good time," Penny told him with a kind of adoration in her eyes. "I'll remember every word of it. I could go on listening for ever."

Richard Arkwright laughed, and looked at her again sideways.

"I wouldn't make you suffer as much as that," he said. "I'm not really a great talker, except when I get going about the Navy and the Merchant Service."

He had to turn to his neighbour at table, whom he had neglected shamefully because of his interest in this American girl who was as pretty as a peach, he thought, and very vital. He would much like to meet her again. He liked her style and he liked the poise of her head, and the humour in her eyes, and the spirit behind them.

She gave him the chance of meeting her again before the meal ended.

"I'd like my family to meet you," she said. "Is there any chance of your being able to spend a week-end with us in a little old house by a big lake, forty miles from Boston? I could take you out in a car, or you could come by train to Taunton, and hire a car from there."

"It's frightfully kind of you," he answered. "I'd like it awfully."

"We have a golf-course at the garden gate," said Penny, hoping it would tempt him. "And if you're keen on riding I'd be glad to ride with you and show you a bit of Massachusetts."

"I say, that sounds splendid!" he answered. "You're sure your people wouldn't think I was butting in?"

"They'd be crazy to have you as a guest."

He went for a week-end and enjoyed himself a good deal it seemed. Out of uniform, in a blue jacket and grey flannel trousers, he looked less heroic in Penny's eyes and more boyish. He played a very good game of golf, she noticed, though not as good as her own. They went riding together through the woods, and then tied up the horses and sat together on the Big Stone overlooking the lake.

"Tell me about England," said Penny, as they sat there in the warm sunlight. "Tell me about the Blitz over London, and how the people live in the shelters, and what is the secret of their wonderful courage."

He hadn't seen much of the Blitz except at Portsmouth where it had been fairly hot. But one night on leave in London he had struck it badly. It was one of the worst nights and he expected to be killed at any moment. He could hear houses and great blocks of flats crashing all round. That was when he had been dining with his Aunt Susan and his cousin Phoebe in the Langham Hotel just opposite the B.B.C.

"I was scared stiff," he told her; "but of course I had to look brave, being in uniform, and in the company of my Aunt Susan—who never turned a hair."

"I don't believe you were a little bit scared," cried Penny, laughing at him. "You can't make me believe that. No, sir!"

"Absolutely true," he told her. "An action at sea was nothing to it. I quaked in every limb."

She refused to believe that he quaked in any part of his body. She had noticed before, she said, that British soldiers and sailors always underestimated their own courage. She had once met a V.C. in Boston, and he had blushed like a schoolgirl when she asked him to tell her how he had won that decoration.

Richard Arkwright laughed at this scepticism.

"You've no idea," he told her. "It's no joke sitting under high-explosive bombs, and hearing the neighbourhood crashing into rubble and ruin. But what beats me is the way the Londoners stuck it at its worst. That night a crowd of old ladies and gentlemen assembled in the lounge of the Langham. They were the old types, now disappearing—old dames of the Edwardian era, old buffers who remembered the Boer War. There they sat with all hell raging round them, talking in quiet voices and behaving very politely to each other. 'Wouldn't you like this footstool, my dear? I'm afraid you're in a draught, old girl.' I watched them with wonderment. And afterwards I went out into the streets and saw the air raid people at work, and the fire-fighters, and the police, and did my best to lend a hand."

"I thought you said you were afraid," interjected Penny.

"Scared stiff!" said Arkwright again. "But those fellows on top had thinned out, or paid a visit to another part of London. There was a policeman who ought to have got two V.C's . . ."

He told a good story about a London policeman. He also told a story about a young woman driving an ambulance through blazing hell, and another about a hospital nurse he had met that night.

"Those are the real people," he said, with deep enthusiasm. "That's the crowd that's winning this war on the Home Front. By God! I take my hat off to them!"

Penny's eyes were wet now and then because of this heroism of the common people.

"I wish I were English!" she cried. "I wish I could have a chance of being over there, instead of living in a land of peace and plenty, with luxury all round me."

"It's better over here," answered Arkwright. "This is the Garden of Eden. I shall be sorry to leave it."

"We're spared too much," said Penny. "We want a good hard knock to shake us out of our self-complacency. We wallow in material comfort. Everybody over here is fighting for more money, more fun, more everything. The radio advertisements are always teasing us to think we want something else and can't be happy till we get it. And when we get it we aren't happy. We want something else. We're building up a mass-produced civilization. The pioneer spirit is gone from us. We're getting soft. Look at me! What do I do that's any good to anybody? I'm just one of the social set of Boston. Miss Hambledon, daughter of Mr. Edward Hambledon of Commonwealth Avenue. A charming débutante. In the marriage market. Oh, it makes me sick! Why can't I be an ambulance girl driving through hell fire?"

Arkwright laughed quietly at this outburst.

"You wouldn't like it," he said. "And I don't think hell fire is necessary for the development of the human soul. War is a nasty mistake. It's very unpleasant, I assure you. If I were an American I would keep out of it—though speaking as an Englishman I should be glad if you came in."

"Gosh!" cried Penny. "I'll go crazy if we don't come in one day. We're disgracing ourselves. We're leaving you to do all the fighting and dying, while we think we're doing fine by Lease-Lend and turning out munitions for other men to use."

She was very much unlike her brother Tiny, who had a different outlook. In her views she was not typical of American girls. She was Penelope Hambledon, and perhaps a throw-back to some other Penelope in Shakespeare's England. She was, thought Richard Arkwright of H.M.S. *Rodney*, the most charming girl he had met in Boston. It was a great treat to stay for a week-end with her family.

It was a great treat for Penny to have him for other week-ends. But it put her in "a bit of a jam," as she called it. For, after several week-ends riding, swimming, playing golf, and walking in the woods with Richard Arkwright of *Rodney*, she knew that he was the man she wanted, if he wanted her. But, meanwhile, she was engaged to a young professor of Harvard, who was seriously in love with her. That was very awkward, she thought. It put her in the hell of a jam.

X

LIEUTENANT RICHARD ARKWRIGHT of *Rodney*, now doing repairs in Boston docks, was astonished at the warmth of American hospitality, but having a good head on his shoulders, was aware that this personal friendliness did not rule out an underlying criticism of England and the English. Sometimes it made him laugh and sometimes it made him angry, though he tried to keep his temper, and mostly did, having a sense of humour and an easy-going nature not quick to take offence.

Criticism was hardly the word for it in the neighbourhood of the Docks. Fighting took place most nights between British and American seamen.

"What's it all about?" he asked his men. "Why can't you keep the peace with these Yanks? Do you go about asking for trouble?"

He had an answer from one of the petty officers.

"It's the Yanks who ask for it. As soon as they see our lads they stop chewing gum, spit on the floor, and make personal remarks about our mothers. That is to say, they call us sons of bitches. If that isn't asking for it, I don't know what is. Well, they get it straight in the jaw, and then the scrap begins."

"A bit of prejudice on both sides, perhaps," suggested Arkwright.

"Quite likely," agreed the petty officer; "but our lads don't like some of the questions put to them in an ugly sort of way. Why the hell does the British Army always get licked? Why the hell did we retreat from Dunkirk and Norway, and every other place, when we met a few Germans? Why didn't we pay our debts after the last war? Why did England always expect Americans to pull her chestnuts out of the fire?

Why the hell didn't we do our own fighting? Our men get vexed, sir."

Arkwright laughed at this mild way of putting it.

"Very crude stuff!" he said. There seems to be a traditional hostility on both sides—a hang-over from ancient history."

"Funny thing is," said the petty officer thoughtfully, "that there's a kind of friendliness at the back of it. They're just curious to see how much our men will take. I can't help feeling that they have an admiration for us in spite of all their ugly words. Get 'em on the side and they're good-humoured fellows and anxious to know things."

"What kind of things?" asked Arkwright.

The petty officer said they wanted to know how Londoners lived under the German bombs. What kind of life was it anyhow for the women and children? What kind of food did they get? What did they do when their homes were knocked out? Why were they so darned heroic? What was the war about, anyway?

"Very intelligent questions," remarked Arkwright, "and damned difficult to answer, Johnson. Now tell your men to go easy with their fists. All the officers are getting worried about this continual scrapping. It doesn't give *Rodney* a good name. It doesn't make for Anglo-American friendship. It's you petty officers who have most influence with the men. Do your best, Johnson."

"Very good, sir. But I don't promise any results. It's become a habit. There was something like a pitched battle last night. Bloody noses on both sides. Of course, we got the best of it as usual. Some of those Yanks were sorry for themselves."

Arkwright laughed again.

"I believe you enjoy it. Damn silly, I call it. Here we are in a friendly country which is pouring out hospitality . . ."

All that was crude stuff, as he said. It was less crude within his own experience, but the criticism crept out here and there and sometimes he was aware of a kind of covert hostility. In the lower ranks he had come across it among taxi-drivers in New York. Pretty crude also, but interesting. One of them had put him down at the Plaza and then started talking.

"British Navy, ain't you?"

"Yes."

"Well, they're doing all right, but we ain't so fond of the British people."

"I'm sorry about that," said Arkwright with a laugh. "What's your grievance?"

"They didn't pay the debt in the last war, and they're trying to get us into this one. Well, we ain't coming into this one. No gratitude last time. Called us Uncle Shylock when we asked for our money."

Arkwright searched his brain for the right answer. He wasn't strong on that.

"We could only pay if you bought our goods," he said; "and you could not take them. It was something like that."

"Not good enough," said the taxi-driver. "Now I'm telling you. I've a son getting on for nineteen. Doing well in a drug store. There's millions of boys like him. We ain't going to let them go overseas to bleed to death in some field in Europe because England is at war with Germany again. What's that got to do with us? And why didn't England keep Hitler from re-arming when there was time enough? Why should we clear up your dirty mess again? Once was too much."

"That's all right," answered Arkwright cheerfully. "We're not asking you to send your boys overseas, though we should like to see them come."

The taxi-driver held out his hand.

"No offence meant," he said; "but it's best to talk straight if one talks."

"I agree with you," said Arkwright.

"And how I've had my say I'll say one thing more. Your civilians have guts. I'll say they have!"

That was the "low down" from the man in the street. Higher up in the social scale they saw it differently.

Some of the officers of H.M.S. *Rodney* were entertained by the Faculty of Columbia University. One of them, speaking across the luncheon-table, was troubled, it seemed, about India.

"Why doesn't your Government give India its freedom? Wouldn't it come into line with your fight for Liberty and Democracy?"

Richard Arkwright had met that one before. Not having been to India, he could not answer with any air of infallibility.

"Haven't we offered them practically self-government?" he asked.

"Not enough to satisfy Mr. Gandhi," answered the professor, pleasantly but ironically.

"That crafty old gentleman is not easily satisfied," answered Arkwright with a laugh.

"I don't want to be critical," said the professor, proceeding to be critical, "but from the American angle it seems strange that Great Britain, which has led the fight for freedom so often, should still keep her Colonies tied to the strings of Whitehall, and exploit four hundred million Indians—and Heaven knows how many natives of Africa—by taxation which keeps them below the bread-line, and in miserable social conditions, while the British aristocracy keeps rich on the proceeds."

The naval lieutenant laughed again.

"I don't profess to know much about these things," he said; "but I don't think your facts are quite right somehow. The British Government doesn't get any revenue out of India. They have their own budget, you know. As for the Colonies, and I suppose you include the Dominions, they broke away from Whitehall a long time ago. I've been to Australia. They have a complete independence and keep rubbing it into any visiting Englishman. Allegiance to the King and a common tradition is the only tie which binds them to the Mother country. Hasn't this war proved that it's still a pretty strong tie?"

The professor, who was a thin man with a sallow complexion, looked unconvinced, and smiled in a superior way, as though humouring a young boy.

"Viewed from the American angle," he said, "Great Britain, for which we all have a romantic affection, has still a long way to go before becoming truly democratic. All this King stuff strikes us as very old-fashioned. It's bound to cause social distinctions and political inequality."

"Think so?" asked Arkwright, good-humouredly.

After that luncheon one of the younger professors came up to him and spoke in a low voice.

"I'm sorry you had to listen to that thin-lipped son of a . . . who sat opposite you. Very hard on you, lieutenant, and darned discourteous to a distinguished guest."

"Not at all," answered Arkwright. "I could take it!"

It was harder to cope with hospitality than with criticism, but he stood up to it with great cheerfulness, and a resilient physique. Some of his friends of H.M.S. *Rodney* were beginning to weaken.

"If this goes on much longer," said Jack Tanner, a fellow-lieutenant, "I shall be unfaithful to my wife, develop cirrhosis of the liver, and be incapable of doing my duty to King and country. Gosh! How many Old-fashioneds did I drink yesterday? I reckoned up to six and then lost count in a hazy dream of smart girls, friendly guys, and endless vistas of glad hands all reaching out to shake my paw. Still, I must say it's a great experience. I wouldn't have missed it for the world."

He was sharing a double bedroom at the Plaza with Richard Arkwright. Breakfast had just been brought in on trolleys by a waiter who spoke broken English with an American accent. Jack Tanner tipped the man a quarter, waited until he was gone, lifted various silver covers, and then laughed.

"It's like a giddy fairy-tale," he said. "Warm little rolls, hot buns, orange juice in ice, oatmeal with creamy milk, bacon and tomatoes, fruit, marmalade, and pints of coffee. Is there a war on here? The answer is in the negative. These people don't know what war is. They wallow